**SUIT Y**

**Susan Mac Nicol**

A Men of London Romance

## BARING THE BEAST

Twenty-five year old Oliver Brown is addicted. Two years ago, he was at the height of his career as "Nicky Star," fashion model, porn actor, partier without peer. Then came the accident. Hiding his scars, both emotional and physical, he's gone into hiding. But fine clothing is some solace. A new suit by Debussy? Better even than a ride on his motorcycle Hulk or all the things he used to give and take on camera.

Enter Leslie Scott, the flamboyant, dark-haired, heel-and-tiny-short-wearing twink sent to deliver Oliver's newest fix. A firecracker, Leslie is dapper, generous, in touch with his feminine side but all man, and as gorgeous as any garment ever made. He makes Oliver dream of ending his reclusion, of recapturing a future forever denied him. But for that to happen, Leslie would have to strip him to the bone. Only then will they rebuild life from the bottom up.

# SUIT YOURSELF

## Susan Mac Nicol

# Boroughs
Publishing Group

www.BOROUGHSPUBLISHINGGROUP.com

PUBLISHER'S NOTE: This is a work of fiction. Names, characters, places and incidents either are the product of the author's imagination or are used fictitiously. Any resemblance to actual events, locales, business establishments or persons, living or dead, is coincidental. Boroughs Publishing Group does not have any control over and does not assume responsibility for author or third-party websites, blogs or critiques or their content.

SUIT YOURSELF
Copyright © 2015 Susan Elaine Mac Nicol

All rights reserved. Unless specifically noted, no part of this publication may be reproduced, scanned, stored in a retrieval system or transmitted in any form or by any means, electronic, mechanical, photocopying, recording, or otherwise, known or hereinafter invented, without the express written permission of Boroughs Publishing Group. The scanning, uploading and distribution of this book via the Internet or by any other means without the permission of Boroughs Publishing Group is illegal and punishable by law. Participation in the piracy of copyrighted materials violates the author's rights.

ISBN 978-1942886-38-9

*This book is dedicated to a very special person, one who has been through the mill recently, yet, as a strong, proud, independent woman she rises above the things life throws at her and is a true blue survivor. Jill Limber, this story is for you.*

# ACKNOWLEDGMENTS

There are so many people to thank for this particular Men In London story that I think it needs its own book. But as that isn't a possibility, here goes. *Takes a deep breath…*

Firstly, to my wonderful editor, Michelle Klayman. In the absence of Jill, my usual partner in crime, due to personal circumstances, Michelle has stepped up to the plate on both *Sight and Sinners* and *Suit Yourself*. They say it's tough for an author to get a new editor and, I think, generally they're right. With Michelle, however, it was simply a case of an old friend taking over and making it seamless and painless, and for that I will be forever thankful.

Then there's the fabulous Johnny O'Connell. He's the cover model for the wonderful man in corset on the cover. Johnny took the time out to perform a personal photo shoot for me and sent me loads of sexy and beautiful pictures. Yes, you'll be seeing more of him…. The one on the cover just blew me away. In my mind, he became Leslie. The funny thing is, Johnny isn't that far away from this quirky character himself. Being an avid corset and heel wearer, Johnny also works in the fashion industry. Having feet in both the vintage and burlesque worlds, and being a pole dancer and performer, Johnny is a true chameleon when it comes to dressing up—or down as the case may be. Thank you for your help and unswerving generosity in helping launch this book with its made-to-order cover.

By the way, those gorgeous red heels and corset are Johnny's own.

To fellow author Nic Starr who won a competition to have herself named in one of my future books as a character. I think becoming gay, male, porn star Nicky Starr was fitting, and I know you enjoy this idea, too. May you live forever in this book.

Finally, to a truly lovely fella, Warren Joseph Allen, who teaches me about gay slang, (I had no idea there were so many euphemisms for the female vagina), drag queens, amuses me daily with his witty sense of humour, is a valued business partner *and* talented, too (oh, in *so* many ways, I won't make you blush telling them all). Warren is the web designer of the Nicky Starr website, having put hours and hours into helping me pull the concept of the site together. I dare say he had a lot of fun too when you see what's on there. He's a number cruncher by day, pole dancer and web designer by night and I think he should have his own Bat signal. If anyone has any ideas on this, please send them to me. I'll have a tee shirt made for him. Love ya madly, Professor.

To my beta readers JP Bilboa and Rita Roberts, who offered some wonderful constructive criticism. As always, ladies, your wisdom and advice is appreciated.

And, of course, to all my wonderful readers and fans out there—and all the bloggers who work tirelessly promoting us all for simply the reward of reading a good story. All I can say is *Thank You*, once again. You're always there for me and I know you've been looking forward to Leslie's story. I hope I did it justice.

## CONTENTS

Chapter 1
Chapter 2
Chapter 3
Chapter 4
Chapter 5
Chapter 6
Chapter 7
Chapter 8
Chapter 9
Chapter 10
Chapter 11
Chapter 12
Chapter 13
Chapter 14
Chapter 15
Chapter 16
Chapter 17
Chapter 18
Chapter 19

About the Author

**SUIT YOURSELF**

# Chapter 1

"That dickwad is so overrated. I hate him. I hope his arse rots and his hole closes up." Leslie Scott scowled as he bit his bottom lip in a fit of pique. He glared at the trim figure on the catwalk mincing along the raised platform.

Beside him, Eddie Tripp snorted in laughter. "Hell, Leslie, I'd hate to be one of your exes. Simon might have been a bit of a douche cheating on you like he did, but even he doesn't deserve that fate worse than death. *My* arse is twitching just thinking about it."

Eddie and Leslie sat at the front of the audience at a swanky London fashion event. Working at a local fashion house providing exclusive men and women's suits, Leslie had been invited to see the latest designs gracing the catwalk. Eddie hadn't particularly wanted to be here at the Mystique Hotel extravaganza on a rare Saturday off, but Leslie had batted his eyelashes and opened his baby blues wide, knowing that Eddie would be powerless to resist.

Gideon, Eddie's boyfriend, had shaken his head at Eddie's capitulation and grinned. "God, Eddie, babe, you are so damn easy…" He'd forestalled Eddie's indignant squawk that he was *so* not with a fierce kiss. Leslie loved seeing his fiery friend rendered speechless even though his heart gave a lurch at the two men being so comfortable together. Leslie really wanted a relationship like theirs.

He narrowed his eyes at the ex-boyfriend now strutting along the catwalk in the posh confines of the Bella Ballroom. Simon Hooper looked as if butter wouldn't melt in his mouth with his platinum-streaked, stylishly coiffed blond hair and pink, full lips, but Leslie had seen that mouth in action on another man's cock and seen Simon's ugly side when he'd been caught out in mid-blow. That pretty mouth could say some fairly hurtful things, like, "Well, I wasn't getting what I needed from yours." That comment had really stung.

"Yes, well, just because he's a model and has everyone fawning over him like he's the next best thing to Michael J Willett means fuck all to me. The man's a bitch." Leslie huffed and waggled perfectly manicured fingers in Eddie's direction.

Eddie grinned. "You look even better than him, honest. I mean…" He paused and stared hard at Simon currently sashaying away from them. He wore a tailored, ruffled pink shirt and tight, plaid green and brown designer trousers emblazoned with the flamboyant Tracy Trey's signature label of a rainbow-coloured chameleon on the pocket. "No one can fault those trousers you have on, and those shoes. You look like a prince, whereas he looks like the frog. A bloody Amazon rainforest frog at that, wearing all those colours." Eddie winced. "I mean, multi-coloured *plaid* trousers? Come on."

Leslie's heart warmed at Eddie's obvious sincerity and he had to admit he probably simpered a little. "Well, I do try my best." He looked down at his black, silky, clinging long-sleeved shirt and tight, sexy bronze silk pants complete with his favourite pair of comfortable heels, a pair of Jimmy Choo peep-toe pumps, just his style. They were slightly scuffed but he'd not said no to them when one of the diva female models had thrown them aside after a fashion show he'd attended and asked him casually if he wanted them. A starving wolf attacking a hunk of premium quality meat had nothing on Leslie as he dove to get them. He'd hissed like a striking salamander at another woman trying to do the same thing. He'd been gratified when she'd backed off.

The only thing irritating him about his outfit was his thong. It just wasn't behaving properly, riding up his backside and into his crack. Leslie didn't mind fingers or tongues doing that, but an errant piece of a fabric was simply a no-no.

Eddie chuckled as Leslie turned out a well-waxed leg and admired the shoe on his slim ankle. "God, you are such a narcissist…"

"Am not," Leslie declared indignantly. "Can I help it that I like good stuff and classy wear? And that it looks great on me?" He huffed and pretended to glower at Eddie from between his lashes. "I can't help it. I have high standards."

"Yeah, you can be a right snob," Eddie retorted. Then seeing the scowl forming on Leslie's face, he grinned. "But I love you anyway." He nudged Leslie's arm with a gangly elbow. "That guy over there can't take his eyes off you. He's been eying you up since we got here."

Leslie's head whipped round so fast he thought he'd given himself whiplash. An admirer was always welcome in his current state of sexual drought. "Who would that—oh, *him*. That's Charlie." His lips curled in derision and he scoffed. "I wouldn't touch him with my pretty eight-inch bargepole. He's into abusing his boyfriends. I know one of his last ones, Sandy, ended up in hospital with a broken nose when that prick over there," he gestured to the thickset, dark-haired man currently looking at Leslie as if he wanted to lick him all over, "took exception to the way he was looking at another bloke. Sandy insisted he wasn't checking him out, but it didn't stop Charlie." He spat the name out, and Eddie reached up to wipe a small bit of spit off his face with a grimace. "He smashed poor Sandy's face into a door frame. He had to have surgery to fix it, 'cos he's an actor."

Eddie's pale face darkened. "Hell, what a fucking bully. Did anyone report him to the police for it?" His green eyes narrowed as he threw Charlie a look, one Charlie obviously saw as he turned to look at the crowd behind him then looked back at Eddie in bafflement, mixed with a little bit of panic.

"No, Sandy wouldn't do it. He just stopped seeing him. The bastard got off scot free." The unfairness of it made Leslie's blood heat. He hated bullies and men who took out their frustrations on someone else. "However, Sandy's new boyfriend, Alex, did corner Charlie in a bathroom a while ago and they had a 'chat.'" He frowned. "I don't know what Alex said to him but there have been no more beatings that I know of. Alex is a bouncer at a nightclub, so I don't think I'd want to mess with him."

Eddie nodded in satisfaction. "Glad someone put him straight." He chuckled. "In a manner of speaking." He threw Leslie a fond glance. "There was something wrong with one of your last statements, Leslie."

Leslie was puzzled. "What statement?"

"Eight inches?" Eddie laughed loudly as Leslie's face heated up. "I've seen it and I'm not sure that's true—"

Leslie pinched Eddie's arm, causing him to yowl in pain. "Shut up. It's my fantasy and you have no right to cast aspersions on it." He grinned back at his friend. "Besides, maybe it's grown since the last time you saw it. I might be going through a growth spurt, you know. I am only twenty-three."

Eddie guffawed. "Yeah, right, you tell yourself that." They both fell quiet as the crowd around started clapping and the auditorium exploded with a spate of quick-paced and rather loud trance music as Tracy Trey walked onto the catwalk with his models. Leslie started clapping with them. Tracy might be a little eccentric, and his plaid wear didn't appeal to Leslie in the least, but he was sheer fucking genius when it came to underwear and sexy corsets, one of his little pleasures. He owned quite a few items with the chameleon logo.

The noise finally died down, and as Tracy Trey strode off the stage, people started to get up and leave. Leslie sighed and stood up. "Come on. I guess you're anxious to get back to that lovely man of yours and fuck his brains out. Or cook something, depending on how you two spend your leisure time."

Eddie pursed his lips as they joined the throng of people leaving the venue, making their way to the exit in front. "Well, in my opinion, there's a way to do both at the same time. One of my favourite pastimes is making my world-renowned double chocolate mousse then smearing it all over Gideon's dick. Then sucking it off. Delicious…" He waggled his eyebrows and Leslie felt his own dick rise at the image of his two friends getting it on in that way.

"Oh," he said enviously. "I imagine that would be a lot of fun. Not that I haven't done something similar before myself, but I've never really had someone *special* to do it with like you…" His voice trailed off and he knew he sounded a little wistful.

Leslie's relationships tended not to last too long. He was honest with himself. He was rather high maintenance and boyfriends either tended to use him as a one-night fuck or got tired of the whole overwhelming Leslie persona and went on to someone easier to be with. Someone more malleable and not as fiery.

They exited the hotel into the chill grey of a January Saturday afternoon. Leslie shivered and wrapped his warm pea coat tighter around his frame.

Eddie's face softened. "Honey, you are a complete catch for the right guy. So far you just haven't found him. You will, though. You're beautiful inside *and* out, and these arseholes you date never seem to realise that." He reached out an arm and hugged Leslie close.

Leslie snuggled into his friend, enjoying this rare PDA. He breathed in Eddie's scent, feeling safe and cherished. "Yes, well, they never stick around long enough. It's all wham, bang, fuck off, Leslie," he muttered against Eddie's shoulder.

Eddie released him and planted a soft kiss on his forehead. "More fool them," he murmured softly. "There's a guy out there for you, I promise. You know I said you were a prince in there? Well, you gotta kiss a lot of frogs before you find him."

He hugged Leslie again then stood back. "Now I'd better get back home, before Gideon finds someone else to lick chocolate off."

Leslie snorted. "That'll be the day. That man adores you. You know that, you shameless hussy."

His friend's facial expression changed to one that Leslie called 'Giddy Goofy.' Dreamy, with a carnal glint to the eyes. In his fanciful moments, Leslie thought perhaps that description sounded like a delicious recipe.

"Yeah, well, I guess it's mutual." He turned to lope down the pavement, waving as he made his way to the tube station across the road. "Speak to you later, Leslie. Thanks for the afternoon and the company."

"No, thank *you*," Leslie called after him. "For putting up with me and a bloody fashion show."

Eddie shot him a wide grin across his shoulder and crossed the street, striding toward home and no doubt Gideon.

## Chapter 2

Leslie watched his friend depart and heaved a sigh. "And there we have it," he muttered. "Alone again."

He started walking, clutching his coat around his shoulders, his underwear still uncomfortable. He'd change it when he got home and throw this beastly thong out. His small but comfortable flat wasn't far, one of the reasons he'd chosen it. It was close to the Mystique Hotel where most of their company fashion events were held. It was also close to his job at Debussy Fashion in Hackney, where he worked as a trainee fabric buyer and general factotum to his rather high-powered and sometimes scary as hell boss, Laverne Debussy-Smith.

Leslie had been living in his new home for three months, ever since both of his previous housemates had moved out of the Kennington house they'd shared. Eddie had of course moved in with Gideon to the palatial flat above their restaurant, Galileo's, and Taylor had moved in his with his fiancé, Draven. Both his housemates had been apologetic about the turn of events and deserting Leslie, but he'd been philosophical about it.

"I knew it would happen one day," he'd sighed when they'd taken turns staring at him with anxious eyes. "I'm really happy for you guys. You deserve this. It's about time I moved my arse and found somewhere closer to work anyway with the amount of time I'm spending there recently. Gives me an excuse to find a nifty flat and put my stamp on it."

Just before Taylor had moved out, they'd given their notice. Taylor's boyfriend Draven had found Leslie somewhere suitable to live, for which he was grateful. He was certainly paying less than he'd expected and suspected Draven had pulled someone's strings. Also, thanks to an unexpected but decent raise from Laverne when hearing of his predicament, Leslie had been able to afford the compact (euphemism for tiny box room, he thought) studio flat in Shoreditch.

Five minutes into his walk home, he passed work and on a sudden impulse, he decided he'd pop in and see if anything was going on. Often there were spare pieces of sample fabric and clothing items left over in the staff recycle bin for them to take home.

Leslie desperately wanted a piece of frilly lace for a fancy dress party he was attending soon. He was going as Adam Ant and needed lacy cuffs sewn onto on his royal blue jacket. Perhaps he might get lucky going into the office when there were not too many eagle-eyed and needy employees around.

He made a quick stop for a coffee at the small café next to work and, as he left, he waved cheekily at the construction workers working on the scaffolding above the café. There was one burly young soul called Frankie whom he rather liked and who always wolf-whistled when he walked past. He wasn't there today but Leslie waved anyway. There were a few hoots and comments and he waggled his arse in return.

Normally he wouldn't have been so flamboyantly camp in the vicinity of what he imagined was mostly a heterosexual encamp—apart from Frankie, who'd made his desire to have Leslie known—but they'd been working there for months and he'd gotten to know them. He was still on the fence about taking Frankie up on his offer. The guy seemed very sweet but a bit innocent. Leslie rather liked them a little more experienced, even older.

Laverne made it a habit to send coffee and cake over to them every now and then to keep them sweet. She was philosophical about the noise and dust that swept through their own offices. "At least if I keep them a bit happy, they're happy to return the favour," she'd said one night. "The other evening, I had an important gentleman from Japan here and they stopped twenty minutes earlier with all the drilling and stuff so I could have my meeting in peace. They scratch my arse, I scratch theirs with treats. It works well."

The lobby of the quaint old office building was quiet, with only the elderly concierge sitting behind the worn, scratched desk as he read his copy of *The Sun*. Stuck on Page 3, Leslie noticed with a grin. The man waved at Leslie, who walked over to the old lift, the one that still had the pull-down metal gate, which creaked ominously as it travelled to the third floor.

"Afternoon, young Larry. You do know it's a weekend, don't you?" He scowled. "Not that them lot next door care. Bloody noisy gits, the lot of them. Why they have to work on a weekend, I don't know."

Leslie sighed as he waved hello. Sid's constant moans at the workforce next door could get a little wearing. "Yes, Sid, I do. I'm just here to check something out."

The concierge insisted on calling him Larry. No amount of conversation to explain that his name was actually Leslie had ever got Sid any closer to remembering it. It was easier to simply accept the name change even though Leslie hated it. It reminded him of a game called Larry the Lounge Lizard his older brother Nathan had used to play years ago.

"Well, beware. The cleaners are working up on your floor, and you know what that young Adrian is like. Bloody handsy little bastard, wasn't he, at the last Christmas party? If I recall, he was all over you like bloody ants on a picnic blanket."

Leslie paused. He did indeed remember that night when Laverne had needed to extricate Adrian's tongue from Leslie's mouth and his greedy fingers from his crotch. Leslie had been a little under the weather that night and his reflexes at fending off unwanted attention had been somewhat impaired. The words 'voracious octopus' sprung to mind.

"Oh, thanks for the warning. I'll do my best to avoid him." Leslie pressed the button for the lift and waited. When it opened, he stepped inside and listened to the sound of cheesy music as the lift arrived at the third floor.

Leslie waited for the doors to open then peered cautiously out into the corridor. It was empty. He tried to tiptoe quietly down the corridor so as to not to attract anyone's attention, and he breathed a sigh of relief when he got to the main office unscathed. He slipped in and closed the door behind him, locking it for good measure. Let Bad Breath Adrian try and get through that, he thought with a smirk. As he turned, someone loomed in front of him and he shrieked like a cat being disembowelled. His heart pounded and he pressed himself back against the door, wondering for an instant if Adrian had found him after all.

"Leslie, dear, really?" Laverne Debussy-Smith's husky voice sounded pained. "My fucking ears are now ringing like the bells of Notre Dame."

"Well, jeez Louise, forgive me for thinking someone was about to murder me," retorted Leslie snarkily, bearing in mind this *was* his boss and trying to tone it down just a bit.

Laverne's Adam's apple bobbed up and down as she drawled, "What are you doing here, anyway? On the scrounge again?" Her words belied the affectionate glance she directed at him as Leslie huffed.

Laverne Debussy-Smith was a law unto herself. She was owner and founder of the company, as well as being a talented clothing designer. Her own suit label, simply titled 'Debussy,' was highly prized, made for both women and men. Leslie had one in his closet but doubted he could ever afford another.

Laverne was also a man who'd been born Lenny James, but decided that Laverne was definitely more fun in the office. The man behind the woman was just as treasured by the staff.

"Ha-ha. If you must know, I was coming in to check that delivery for Monday. The suit for that guy in Waterloo, the one who spent a bloody fortune on it. Oliver somebody or the other." Leslie felt gratified that he'd remembered the delivery he was supposed to do and could use it as an excuse. Laverne's comment about scrounging had rather wounded him, even if it *was* true.

Laverne nodded and Leslie didn't like the glint in her aqua eyes. It looked…cunning. That could be a bad sign of things to come, knowing her. He moved away from the door, going toward the open-plan office, and, coincidentally, the recycle bin.

"Not so fast, my little bit of sex on legs." Laverne's tone became playful and sexy and Leslie's stomach plummeted. He just knew he wasn't going to be investigating the bin for his lace anytime soon from the sound of it. Slowly, he turned to face the woman dressed in a form-hugging, deep blue tailored pants suit, mock breasts pushing up the stressed fabric. Leslie wondered idly if it was screaming for release as the mounds pressed against it like sponge being forced through the fabric tear of a stuffed animal. A ripple of apprehension flooded his body. Laverne's favours came in two distinct flavours. One was the innocuous, 'Could you make me a cup of tea, darling?' to 'Could you just rip your first born from your womb and give it to me?' There was no in-between in Leslie's opinion. Perhaps he was being a bit of a drama queen but these ad hoc requests always made him nervous.

"What?" He sighed resignedly. "What do you need?"

Laverne's handsome, square-jawed face beamed at him from under a wig of silver-blonde thick hair and Leslie thought not for the first time that Lenny made rather a lovely woman. Tall, broad-shouldered, statuesque, and beautifully dressed no matter what, Laverne was a force to be reckoned with and Leslie would do anything for her.

"Well, this must be divine intervention." Laverne prowled her way across to Leslie, who took a deep breath. More than once he'd been embraced between the twin peaks that made up Laverne's chest and every time had been a pretty suffocating experience. However, this time he was given a reprieve.

"The client called and said Monday was no longer good for him, so could I please see whether I could get anyone out there today. I was going to call Charlie and see if he could do it, but now you're here in person, my sweet lad, I rather think Mr. Brown can be all yours."

Leslie raised a perfectly plucked eyebrow. "Really? His name is Oliver Brown? That's pretty bleh. I think I'd die from self-boredom with a name like that." He was relieved at the extent of the favour though. It sounded innocuous enough.

Laverne frowned. "Now, now, don't be a bitch. I mean, what's so great about the name Leslie Scott?"

Leslie spluttered. "Leslie *Tiberius* Scott, if you please."

Laverne stared at him then broke out into great guffaws of laughter that definitely made her the man she was beneath the armour. "Oh my God, Leslie, my little chicken. Tiberius? That is not a name I would associate with a gorgeous Tinkerbell like you. The name Tiberius conjures up hunky Captain James T. Kirk." She licked her lips lasciviously.

Leslie wanted to swear and tell Laverne he was not Tinkerbell, but this was Laverne. And she *had* said gorgeous. Instead, he clenched his teeth and took the comment on the chin.

"Well, at least it's pretty unusual. Not like Oliver Brown."

Laverne must have picked up on the slight hurt in his voice because she sailed over to him and enveloped him in her bosom. It looked like Leslie wasn't getting off scot free tonight.

"Leslie. When I call you Tinkerbell, I mean that I see beauty, grace, and a warm-hearted, beautiful soul. I see big blue eyes, pale skin and black hair that'd make a man's heart melt. I don't see a man who is a fairy, or unable to stand up for himself. You, Leslie

Tiberius Scott, are a wonderful human being and that's why I call you Tinkerbell."

Somewhat mollified, Leslie managed to extricate himself from Laverne's clutches. His hair was mussed from being held so close, but for once, he didn't mind the unruly state of it.

"Well, that's okay then. It's just everyone thinks I'm this slim twink who can't say boo to a goose, and I promise you, I have my moments." He recalled one moment fondly when he'd attacked a man while wearing his high heels then proceeded to bash said dickhead with the end of them. Eddie had been the unfortunate victim that night of the man's unwelcome advances, but between them, Leslie and Taylor had saved the day.

"I have no doubt of that." Lavern's lips twitched as if holding back a smile and then she was back to business. "So, you'll take Mr. Brown's suit to him then, this afternoon? You can take the car. It's not too far away and I think he said he had off-road parking." She waggled a large finger at him. "Mr. Brown is my best customer. You treat him right." She winked. "And I'm really interested to know what the man behind the sexy voice looks like. I've never met him myself."

Leslie sighed. He and the thong could do this. "Fine. I'll be on my best behaviour, I promise. Let me get the suit from the Arbour and I'll load it in the car." He looked at her hopefully. "I want to change, too." He looked down at his glad rags. "These aren't particularly *suitable* for delivering a suit." He snorted at his own wit.

Laverne rolled her eyes. "There are some spec suits in the back, change into one of those. I've no doubt I'll ever see it again." Spec or specimen suits were ones that Laverne had made but were deigned not good enough for sale even though in Leslie's eyes they were perfect.

Leslie batted his eyelashes. "You mean I get to keep it? Oh, Laverne. You doll. I don't suppose you have spare underwear anywhere, do you?" He wriggled uncomfortably. "This damn string is chafing my backside."

Laverne shook her head. "No, sweets, I don't have any Andrew Christians or fancy thongs lying around. You'll either have to go commando or wear the one you have on. Now be off with you, urchin. Post haste. The Arbour awaits."

The Arbour was the room where all the suits that were already made were stored. It was nothing more than a very large, high-ceilinged and airy room with rails and hangers around the walls and a large olive tree in the centre, hence the name. Laverne was fond of olive trees and this one was close to eight feet, set into glistening white pebbles in an enclosure set into the laminated floor. It was looked after as if it were a precious baby. They'd even held office picnics around its spreading branches.

"I hope the car has petrol," Leslie grumbled as he turned the knob to go out to the door, forgetting he'd locked it. He turned the key impatiently and yanked the door open.

"It's all fuelled up," Laverne promised. "Thank you, Leslie, I owe you one. Be careful how you go now and bring the car back safely." Her tone held a warning. The last time Leslie had used a company asset he'd put the wrong fuel in it and had to call out the Automobile Association to rescue him. The cost had not gone down well with the rather tight-fisted Laverne.

It was on the tip of Leslie's tongue to say he'd take payment of some French lace in return for having his Saturday afternoon stuffed up, but he thought the better of it. He'd have a look in the bin when he brought the car back later and hopefully by then he'd be alone to rummage. Rather let Laverne think she had a debt to pay. Perhaps he could get a Friday off sometime soon and go to Brighton for the weekend. He had a good friend down there who'd be happy to take him out on the town.

Laverne's voice interrupted his musings.

"Text me when you're done and let you know you've made it out of the house alive. I mean, you never know, he might decide to keep you. I would."

At first, Leslie felt a twinge of unease at that thought; then random images of being tied up like an old-school heroine and ravaged by a handsome stranger flitted through his mind.

*Hmm, actually that doesn't sound so bad.*

Agreeing that he would text Laverne when he was done, and happy he had something to do this afternoon instead of being home alone (and how sad was that), Leslie whistled as he strutted down the corridor to the Arbour, keeping an anxious eye out for pervy Adrian.

He'd go and see the boringly named Mr. Brown, deliver his suit and then—who knew. Perhaps he'd take himself off to a club tonight and dance the night away. He might even meet someone and go home or be taken home for some heart-stopping, sweaty sex. Of course, waking up with the man tomorrow still in his bed would be a bonus. Cuddling was one of Leslie's favourite pastimes and he didn't get to do it often enough.

He changed into a rather nifty suit and a tailored shirt, and grimaced at the fact he'd have to keep the thong on. He wasn't visiting a customer with his balls hanging out. He found himself a pair of much more comfortable and more respectable shoes to wear; they just happened to be a pair of Armani Loafers.

He whistled as he put them on. His Choos and the rest of his own outfit were popped in a bag and held close, not wanting to let them out of his sight. He grinned when he remembered his boss's comment about not getting it back. She knew him so well. Some of his best outfits were 'borrowed.'

## Chapter 3

The customer's house resided in a cul-de-sac in the middle of the respectable area of Waterloo. Bare-branched trees jutted starkly up from the pavement, which framed clusters of bungalows and double-storey houses set back from the road. They all appeared to have the requisite postage stamp front gardens.

Leslie parked on the wide kerb—a real bonus in his book as he was used to parking on busy streets with double yellow lines (and getting tickets)—unfolded his legs out of the little red Ford Ka he'd borrowed from work, and stood to observe the place with a jaded eye.

It was a seemingly palatial but grubby white-painted house with an ornate wooden front door, which was set with a bevelled paned glass window. A weed-strewn driveway led up to the house, and the gardens surrounding the place looked overgrown and unloved. In its heyday, it must have been quite something. Now, in its current state, even the house seemed to match the name 'Brown.' Ordinary, boring and *so* totally lacking in originality. A tickle of guilt passed through his slender frame as he thought perhaps Eddie and Taylor might have a point when they called him a snob. He shook that off with the thought that *he* still preferred to say he had high standards.

He felt a twinge of sympathy for the poor, neglected camellia valiantly fighting its way up from what looked like a clump of thistles. He was rather partial to camellias, having once had an older lover who'd filled a bathtub with the pink blooms and champagne and seduced Leslie into it with one sexy strip of his clothing and a promise of an earth-shattering blowjob. Said lover was now deceased, unfortunately, having had a heart attack when his wife confronted him with the evidence of his various *off-piste* affairs with young men. However, Leslie still thought fondly of Ralphie at moments like these.

He tut-tutted as he opened his boot and removed the enclosed grey suit, giving it a loving caress as he folded it gently over his left forearm.

"There we go, sweetie. I'm not sure why someone who lives in an unkempt house like this needs a suit like you. You're far too lovely for a place like this. I hope he takes care of you."

He picked up his leather business folder and secured it under his other arm. Taking a deep breath, he adjusted his thong, which had once again ridden up between his cheeks. He strode confidently up to the front door, narrowly avoiding what looked like dog crap on a paving stone covered with dead grass as he did. He stopped and frowned down at the offending item.

"You dare get one bit of your smelly self on my Armani loafers and you are toast," he hissed at what he now saw was simply a clump of dried mud. Delicately avoiding all other ground-strewn landmines, he managed to get to the front door. He shook his head at seeing there was only a broken bell with wires hanging out looking sorry for itself, and he raised a hand—neither of which was truly free—to try and knock on the door as hard as he could.

He waited.

The inside of the house was silent. There was no scuffling down what he imagined were worn stairs, no clatter of shoes across laminated floors and no welcoming opening of the door to greet him. He frowned and knocked again, louder this time. His folder slipped from where it was secured under his arm and he quickly tightened his arm to hold it in place.

"Hello? Mr. Brown, are you home? My name is Leslie Scott and I'm here with your new suit," he announced grandly.

He wriggled his backside uncomfortably—that damn thong, what the hell was wrong with it—and scowled as he raised a hand to knock again. As he did so, the door opened. A man's face peered out of him, half hidden. It was dark inside but what Leslie could see of the face looked rather tasty. That was the first surprise of this visit.

A shock of shaggy, honey-blond hair hung over Mr. Brown's forehead, and his tanned skin, neat beard and stubble and one wide amber eye all mingled together to make Leslie feel much better about his customer delivery. Mr. Brown also looked a little familiar.

Leslie gave the man what he knew was a dazzling smile, as he'd been praised for it more than once, and indicated the suit hanging across his right arm.

"Mr. Brown? I'm from Debussy Fashion. I'm here to deliver the suit you ordered."

The man looked a little taken aback, but the door didn't open any wider. "Oh, I see." His well-modulated voice sounded a little strained. "Ermm, perhaps you could hand it over to me?" An arm covered in the faintest blond hair and ending in long, slender fingers with well-kept nails reached out of the door, clearly intent on Leslie pressing the suit into his hand.

The whole thing reminded Leslie of YouTube videos of Salad Fingers, something he was addicted to. He shook his head vehemently. "I really need to come in and get the delivery receipt signed, plus you might like to try it on before I leave, make sure it fits?"

The door wobbled to and fro as Mr. Brown indicated his refusal of such a kind offer. "Oh no, I won't be trying it on. There's really no need for that. Do you really need to come in?" His voice seemed hopeful that the answer would be no.

Leslie sighed. He was starting to think he didn't really want to go in there with a man who seemed a little, well, strange, but he knew Laverne would have a hissy fit if he didn't. "I'm afraid I do need the paperwork signed, yes. I won't take up much of your time, I promise."

There was silence and Leslie shuffled from one designer-clad foot to the other in impatience. It was rather chilly outside and his steadily rising nipples chafed underneath his snugly tailored shirt. Finally, Mr. Brown conceded defeat as the door opened wider and a hand swung behind him, bidding Leslie to enter.

Despite his coat, Leslie shivered as he stepped inside. It was lighter now, and he could see the faint glow of lamps from a room to his left. The air was warm and fragranced with sandalwood. He stood with the suit still draped over his arm and raised an enquiring eyebrow as Mr. Brown remained mute in the small entrance hall.

Now that he was closer, Leslie took stock of the man.

His first impressions had been correct: the man *was* attractive. A couple of years older than him, he guessed, and a little taller, his customer had broad shoulders that were encased in a snug-fitting long sleeved dark green shirt. His narrow, tapered waist was evident in his loose chinos, with legs that were muscular and well defined. Mr. Brown's dark blond hair was long, shoulder-length strands falling like a curtain over the right side of his face, obscuring the full view. His square chin and cheeks were covered in thick, light blond stubble and one eye gazed at him curiously and with a modicum of trepidation. Leslie had to say, he approved, but he wished he could see the man's face properly. He was sure he knew him from somewhere.

"Do I know you?" he asked contemplatively. "Perhaps you've been into the business in person and I've seen you there?"

Leslie didn't imagine the shutter coming down on his customer's face as he turned away and motioned Leslie into the lounge on the side of the hallway.

"I doubt it. I haven't been to the fashion house, I'm afraid. Please, come into the lounge and you can leave the suit there. You said you had paperwork to sign?" His tone indicated that he wanted to get this ordeal over as soon as possible.

"Yes, just the delivery receipt. It's in my folder. Where would you like me to put the suit?" He stopped dead and stared wide-eyed around the inside of the lounge. Clearly, appearances were indeed deceiving. The interior was beautifully and tastefully decorated in shades of cream and amber, splashes of colour populating the eye-catching overall canvas of the room in the form of a multitude of cushions on the large buttermilk-coloured couch. Bright, rainbow-coloured paintings reminiscent of Matisse dotted the walls. Plants were in abundance, green foliage spreading wide and welcoming arms; Leslie felt as if he was in some alternate tropical resort. He expected a bird of paradise or a toucan to whizz past his head at any moment.

"Fuck me. This room is bloody gorgeous," he exclaimed then winced as he realised he'd just sworn in front of a client. Laverne would have his balls if she found out. "Err, I'm sorry about the language, I—"

Oliver Brown gave a quiet laugh and waved a hand around the room. "No worries. I've heard the word before, believe me." His tone was dry. "I'm glad you like it. It's my little bit of fantasy living."

Leslie nodded. "Well, it works for me. Uhmm, where do you want me to put the suit?"

Oliver motioned to the back of the couch. "Just lay it across there, and I'll get that paperwork signed for you. Let me go get a pen. I have one in the kitchen." He disappeared out into the hallway again while Leslie laid the suit down reverently, not feeling too bad about its new home now he'd met the man and seen inside his house. He placed his cherished leather folder on the side table as he took another chance to inspect the room, marvelling at the décor—until something distracted him, something that was easily done as he had the attention span of a two-year-old.

"This fucking thong," he cursed loudly as he reached a hand down into the back of his suit pants and tried to remove the stringed offender from his chafing crack. He was so busy with his bout of arse calisthenics that it was only when he heard a polite cough that he looked up to see a flushed, yet slightly amused half-face observing him. Oliver Brown's dark eye—why on earth had Leslie ever thought that name was boring?—obviously found something funny. Or perhaps he was turned on? There was a hungry look in his eye.

Leslie huffed as his face went pink both with the exertion and the embarrassment of being caught with his own hands down his trousers.

"Is everything all right?" Oliver enquired, his face politely schooled. Leslie waved one airy hand, still fidgeting with the other.

"Oh yes, just having a bit of trouble; I seem to have the wrong thong on." Oliver's eyebrow rose ever so slightly and Leslie hastened to explain.

"I mean it's mine, of course, God knows I wouldn't wear anyone else's—but I have one that I thought I'd gotten rid of for exactly this reason and obviously I hadn't. I think this is the *one*!" He ran out of steam at the precise moment when the problem item resolved itself—for now—and he stood looking at Oliver, unsure what else to say. Gamely, he removed his hand out of the back of his pants.

Oliver nodded wisely. "Ah, thongs. Nasty little hobbits, they are." An uncanny mimicry of Gollum left those beautiful full lips and sounded like the real thing.

Leslie blinked. "Wow. That was a damn good impression."

Oliver shrugged modestly. "A talent, I guess. Not that it will do me any good." His voice was bitter and Leslie suddenly had a burning desire to know what this man's story was—not to mention seeing his whole face.

Being constantly confronted with half a man's visage was strangely disquieting in a *Phantom of the Opera* way. He'd noticed that Oliver was careful to keep the hidden side away as much as possible and that where evident, his hair was artfully draped over it.

The tantalising knowledge that Leslie was sure he'd seen this man before also was playing havoc with his natural curiosity.

Leslie realised he was staring when Oliver waggled a hand in front of his face and addressed him. "Hello, anyone in there? Could I have the paperwork I need to sign please?"

He sounded a little testy. Leslie reached out for the pen in a bit of a panic that he'd been caught drooling over a client and as he did, his quick action knocked it out of Oliver's hand. It went flying across the floor and rolled under the couch.

Oliver sighed with exasperation. "Great. Let me get that for you, shall I?"

He placed his hand on the arm of the couch, and bent down to retrieve the pen. As he did so, his shirt rode up above his waist, exposing the small of his back and Leslie really couldn't help checking it out.

Oliver's honey-hued skin was smooth and the tautness of his chinos enhanced his rounded arse. Leslie nodded in appreciation then, as he saw something he really hadn't expected to see, his jaw dropped and a flash of recognition rushed through his body.

Mouth before brain. "Oh my God, I'd know that tramp stamp anywhere. I've seen it often enough. You're Nicky Starr, the porn actor."

Pen in hand as he straightened, Oliver Brown turned around slowly. His hand unconsciously arranged his hair across the right side of his face. But it was the look on what could be seen of that face that shook Leslie. Composed of panic and anger, but mostly quiet resignation.

They gazed at each other in silence until Leslie blurted out what was on his mind as he tended to do when he was nervous.

"Sorry about the tramp stamp comment."

Leslie seemed to be apologising to this man a lot. "But that tattoo is pretty unique, so I knew it was you. I know it's been a couple of years since you made any new movies, but it all clicked in my brain when I saw it. You look quite different now what with the long hair and beard."

The tattoo was indeed one of a kind from what Leslie knew. Beautifully detailed and imaginatively drawn, the two-inch-tall image of Yggdrasil, the tree of life, had captured Leslie's eye as he'd watched the man before him perform in more porn sessions that he could remember.

Nicky Starr had been his hero and his man crush (along with others of course, but Nicky had been his favourite). Now the man who'd given him a lot of wet dreams and masturbation material was standing before him.

Leslie continued gushing. "You've been gone, what, nearly two years? I was devastated when you retired. I mean, you're so young…" His voice trailed off as he realised Oliver Brown really didn't seem happy at all that he'd been discovered.

Oliver moved away and turned to look out of the window. His hands trembled. "Are you going to call the newspapers? The radio station perhaps, tell them they have an ex-porn star in their midst?" His voice was rough. "Get your moment of fame by telling everyone where I've been hiding out?"

Leslie stared at him in horror and more than a little growing fury that he was being accused of something so underhanded. "What? No, of course not. Why would I do that?"

Oliver shrugged but still didn't turn around. "Everybody does." His tone was flat but Leslie saw his shoulders stiffen. The man looked as if he was barely holding it together.

"Well, I'm not everybody. So don't taint me with the brush that other arseholes use." He knew that last comment didn't really make much sense but he was upset.

Oliver turned slowly, his tone a little less hostile when he spoke. "I'm sorry. Sometimes it's not easy for me to trust people."

"Yeah, well, I know that feeling," Leslie muttered. "I had a boyfriend who cheated on me for weeks until I found him with his mouth wrapped around a stranger's cock. So I'm a little wary myself." He warmed to his subject. "And this one time, there was this party I went to, where I got a bit drunk, and some of the guys I thought were my friends, decided I'd be good for a gang bang. Luckily a real friend of mine saw I was in trouble and helped me out. But that could have been one nasty night."

Oliver blinked. "You seem to have led quite an eventful life," he murmured, but his face was more relaxed now.

"Not like yours, though." Leslie waved his hands around like a puppet on a string. "I mean, you had it all, hot guys to screw, the high life, all those great parties and then one day you just disappeared. Nobody knew where you'd gone. I nearly cried when you stopped making films. You were one of my all-time favourites."

Oliver's face darkened and a look of intense sadness washed across his golden skin like a gentle wave. "Sometimes we don't have a choice," he said quietly. "I'm not particularly newsworthy any more, but I want my privacy."

Leslie's heart ached and he moved closer to Oliver. He took a deep breath and laid a hand on his arm. "Not being forward or anything, and I know you're a customer and all, but you look like you could use a friend, or maybe a hug."

Panic flared in Oliver's face and he stepped back. "That won't be necessary."

For a moment the two men stared at each other and Leslie felt the spark that flared between them. Oliver was definitely attracted to him—that much was obvious from the look in his eye and the quick glances at Leslie's lips, where Leslie's groin was enjoying the attention, too, as his dick inflated.

*Damn thong, it feels like a bloody boa constrictor has my dick. But fuckity fuck. What I can see of this man is simply beautiful. And knowing I've seen him* and *his cock in all their glory isn't helping.*

Leslie's discomfort and porn action reminiscences were forgotten as Oliver moved closer and held out his hand, silently indicating the pen and miming a writing action.

Leslie blinked at it and then with a shrug, he picked up his folder and took out the delivery document. He handed it to Oliver who didn't even read it, simply scribbled a signature across the bottom and handed it back.

"Thank you for delivering my suit," he said, his voice strained. "I appreciate that you came all this way out to do it."

The dismissive tone hurt Leslie, who was simply trying to be nice to someone who looked like he needed a shoulder to cry on.

He decided to throw caution to the wind and ignore the vibes of 'Please leave now' that emanated from his customer. It had worked for him before. He was used to people giving in from the force of his obstinacy and 'I'm here, so you'd better get used to me' personality.

"Where did you disappear to, anyway? The newspapers just said you'd retired due to personal reasons. I searched the Internet for months looking for news on you, but I never found anything. Well, apart from a small article that you'd recently had a bike accident but were recovering well. I was going to send you flowers but I couldn't find out where you lived, or which hospital you were in. I rang your agent but they wouldn't tell me anything either."

He ran out of steam and felt a sense of disquiet at declaring himself to be a stalker of note. Oh, God. Perhaps Oliver would have him arrested now and he'd have to spend the night in a smelly cell filled with sexual deviants who'd see him as some sort of twinky glory hole. That thought caused goose bumps to form on his skin and he shivered. Sometimes his overactive imagination was his own worst enemy.

"You've gone very pale," Oliver said cautiously. "Are you okay?"

Leslie was gratified that Oliver had noticed his predicament. "Just wondering how I'd fight off all the bears that wanted to do me in prison," he explained, seeing Oliver's eyes widen in surprise. "I mean, I'm not bad looking, and I doubt I'd last long in there."

Oliver blinked. The man seemed at a loss for words.

"Because it might have sounded like I was, you know, stalking you," Leslie gabbled. "I wasn't really. I was just worried about you. I'd hate to be arrested for caring about someone."

Oliver found his voice and Leslie was pleased to see the start of what looked like a grin on his half face. "I won't be calling the police, I promise. Well, unless it's one of those stripper grams with a night stick."

Leslie snorted then raised a hand to his mouth, mortified. "Oh, God, sorry. I don't usually do that. I think it's just you bringing out the snort in me."

Oliver definitely grinned now, a wide, easy sight that made Leslie's heart speed up and his toes curl. "It was a pretty adorable snort."

Leslie's cock swelled at the compliment and the fact Oliver thought it had been 'adorable.' The thong took its revenge by wrapping silky fingers around him and squeezing. He winced. He wanted nothing more than to take off his trousers and remove the damn thing, but he had a distinct feeling that would definitely get him arrested. Manfully he ignored his restricted nether regions.

"Glad you liked it. I'm sure I have a few more left in me in case you want to hear them?" He cocked his head enquiringly. "You just have to say something else funny."

Oliver's face relaxed. He seemed to be getting over his earlier mood of 'Fuck off out of my house.'

"You're an unusual man, Leslie. I've never met anyone quite like you."

Leslie's face warmed. "I suppose there are worse things to be called than unusual. Thanks." His hands grew animated. "My all-time favourite was that scene where you were the country gentleman and you found that gypsy lad stealing apples from your orchard. *Fruity Encounter* I think it was called. The way you managed that situation was classic. I wished I was that wicked gypsy."

He fondly remembered jacking off to that scene over and over again as the gypsy lad was ravished to within an inch of his life and enjoyed every minute of it. It had been hot, dirty and as sexy as hell. Oliver was a pretty impressive guy down below.

Oliver nodded. "That was me and Leo Loving," he mused, his face pinking delightfully with the recollection. "He was beautiful, inside and out. He's directing his own films now. Serious films too, not porn. He's done really well for himself."

"Oh, he's wonderful," Leslie gushed. "And I remember you and Gregori Golovin. You two had such great on-screen chemistry. Weren't you both an item at some time? Whatever happened to him?"

Oliver's face darkened. "I haven't seen him in a long time. And we're definitely no longer any sort of 'item.'"

From the look on Oliver's face, Leslie knew he'd struck a nerve. He hastened to fix his faux pas. "So why did you stop? Why aren't you doing something else? You had the talent and contacts to do anything you wanted."

The other man turned to face the picture window and gazed out into the garden. Leslie moved up behind him. He had a suspicion he was wearing Oliver Brown down.

"Honestly, Oliver, you look like you could use someone to talk to," he murmured softly, growing more confident to the point of resting a hand on Oliver's shoulder. "And I'm a good listener."

He waited with bated breath for his hand to be shoved off Oliver's shoulder and to be told to go to hell, but all he heard was a deep sigh, a heart-wrenching one that made his soul weep. It was not short of despair.

When Oliver turned, Leslie moved backwards and watched in apprehension as Oliver drew back the shock of hair covering the right side of face. Leslie's horrified gasp sounded loud in the stillness that followed.

Oliver spoke, his tone weary. "You did ask."

A deep, jagged scar marred the tanned skin of Oliver's face. It was about an inch in width, tapering down from the hairline at his forehead to the bottom of his jaw.

While it was healed and a dark pink in colour, it cast a heavy pall on the beauty of his face; his partial beard covered some of it. Various small pockmarks decorated his cheek and jawline like flecks of silver and his right eye drooped slightly on the outside corner. It gave him a strangely oriental look.

"Oh. My. God," Leslie stammered. "What the fuck happened to you?" He couldn't help feeling a spurt of horror in his stomach that one of his heroes should be so tarnished.

Oliver let his hair fall back across his disfigurement. "Motorbike accident."

"Wow. That must have really hurt. I had no idea…" Leslie's voice tailed off. He really didn't know how to express what he was feeling right now. "I can see why you wear your hair over it..." He bit his lips, seeing the look of derision crossing Oliver's features. He had the sinking feeling his reaction had been what Oliver had expected. Now he'd got it, his earlier seemingly more approachable demeanour soured.

"I was stupid and this was the result." Oliver said curtly. "And afterward no one wanted to fuck or be fucked by me so I was washed up in the porn industry. Apparently they were all squeamish about seeing *this* face in the throes of passion, along with the other scars on my body." His bitter tone bled into the room with the acidity of snake venom.

"So now you know. Don't worry. I'm used to it by now. It's why I don't go out much. I can't stand the pity and disgust in people's faces if my hair blows the wrong way."

"I'm not disgusted," Leslie managed to blurt out. "It was just a bit of a shock. I mean, you were so beautiful…"

Again he knew he'd said the wrong thing by the way Oliver's face hardened and the shutters came down again.

"Yes, because having a scar on my face really changes who I am inside," he spat out. His eyes were both angry and disappointed. "I think the freak show is over now. You should leave."

Leslie tried to smooth things over. "Surely you could have stayed in the industry? Perhaps they could have just shot different camera angles, or left your face out of the shots?"

From the black look on Oliver's face, his efforts had backfired. "What the hell? You mean I should have laid down on the bed or whatever and let some guy screw me from behind all the time so no one gets to see my face?" Oliver was scathing.

Leslie's face flushed and he wanted to crawl into a deep, dark hole. That hadn't been the most intelligent thing he'd ever said, he supposed. But he *had* only been trying to help.

"Thank you for delivering my suit, Mr. Scott." Oliver waved toward the front door. "Have a safe journey home or back to the office, or wherever you're going."

Leslie hurried over to the table, picked up his folder and tucked it under his arm. He felt a little sick at how the day had ended when it had started so promisingly. Perhaps he'd send a Jacqui Lawson *Sorry I was such a prat* greeting card later to the man. He didn't know whether that category existed, but in his opinion, it should. He might have to email Jacqui and tell her about his new idea.

"I'm sorry if I offended you in any way. I didn't mean to," he said softly as he opened the door then turned to look at Oliver. "I'm really glad I met you and found out that you're all right. I was really worried about you disappearing like that. I hope you stay well and uhmm, enjoy the suit."

Oliver's face remained impassive although his jaw twitched, and his fingers clenched and unclenched by his side. With one last smile, which Leslie hoped conveyed his apologies once again, he left the house, closing the door gently behind him.

# Chapter 4

Oliver slumped against the closed door, his weary sigh echoing in the now quiet entrance.

*Why the fuck did I do that?*

His regret at having shown his damaged face to that beautiful, exotic specimen of manhood that was Leslie Scott made his stomach roil and his face heat up in embarrassment.

It was a weakness born of loneliness, his inner voice chided.

*I push everyone away from me, don't get involved, and then all it takes for me to renege on the promise I made to myself is a black-haired, blue-eyed, incredibly fragranced creature that makes my heart beat faster. A man I wanted to drag into the bedroom to make our own porn movie. My personal fantasy come to life.*

In truth, at the first sight of seeing Leslie Scott on his doorstep, Oliver's heart had leapt like a floundering fish and his rather neglected cock had come to life and made its sad presence known.

For a man who'd once made his living with his dick, Oliver certainly wasn't earning any pennies now. His sexual relations with other men were reduced to the occasional discreet escort from an agency he used, plus an occasional fuck with an old friend, Maxwell Lewis, an air steward who visited when he flew into London on one of his whistle-stop stay-overs.

Max was fun, drop-dead gorgeous and rather kinky, and Oliver enjoyed his company. Max was now on a busier overseas route flying in and out of Heathrow, so opportunities to hook up were few and far between.

Oliver was a bit of a hermit. If he had to go out, he'd go to places where the public wouldn't recognise him, or where it was dark. His small circle of friends, who kept his situation private, was his first choice. Then there was this house—both his haven and his prison, a place where he could hide away without the paparazzi and nosey parkers.

His London apartment was known to everyone, so it was currently hired out to some socialite who was regularly in the news. Going to gay clubs to dance and meet people was out of the question; the chances were someone would recognise him and the whole sorry story would have to be told over and over again.

Then Leslie Scott had inveigled his way into Oliver's staid and boring existence. Looking like an exotic bird with his deep blue eyes, fashionably dressed plumage—*that suit he'd worn had been amazing, the lithe body in it even more so*—and a slender, trim-toned body of the type that Oliver hungered after.

Leslie's attempts at trying to cheer Oliver up had been heart-warming and unexpected; his reaction at seeing Oliver's scars for the first time, however, wasn't. Oliver had seen the pity and horror in those sapphire eyes. Leslie hadn't really deserved the contempt Oliver had thrown at him, but he was tired of people's disgust and commiserations.

*I fucked up my face and body not my brain, or my personality. I'm still the same person inside.*

Thinking of that reminded him of Gregori. Leslie's careless question had cut deep. It had hurt having the love of your life walk out on you *again* after seeing you for the first time in the hospital looking less than pretty.

Oliver's mobile rung, and wearily, he pushed himself off the back of the door and went to the dining room to see who was calling.

He smiled slightly when he saw who it was. "Afternoon, Katie," he said. "How goes it with you?"

A loud, angry, southern U.S. twang assaulted his eardrums. He winced.

"Don't you 'Afternoon, Katie' me, you bastard. Where the hell are you? You're supposed to be here at Fidalgo's, having afternoon tea with me. I've been waiting an hour. Are you on your way?"

Oliver's skin prickled with unease. "No, I'm, er, I'm still at home." Shit. He'd forgotten all about this *tea party*. His best friend went quiet. That was when Oliver knew he was *really* in trouble.

Katie Elizabeth Fotheringham was a force of nature—the offspring of a tornado mated with a tsunami—wrapped in a statuesque, busty, and *in your face* package of Southern belle and old English money.

"You're still at home, leaving me here to sit on my own, looking like some poor girl a fella just jilted at the altar?" Her accent was more pronounced now, a sure sign she was getting fired up for the finale, which was to dress Oliver down fiercely with a side order of *fuck you*.

"I got a bit sidetracked, I had this delivery—" Oliver's ear nearly bled at the shriek that emanated from the phone. He'd deliberately left out the word 'suit' as he knew what Katie would say. And he certainly wasn't going to tell her about the hot piece of tail he'd just met. She'd never give up convincing him to 'go for it.'

"Oliver, you didn't. Another damned suit? Honey child, what on earth are you doing? You have a whole room full of new suits you've never even worn."

Oliver blushed. It was true; he was what Katie laughing called *a closet suitaholic*. He craved suits. He'd worn them extensively as Nicky Starr when he'd modelled in his past life, and taken great pleasure in feeling the fabric against his skin; selecting a tie and cufflinks to go with his chosen attire and strutting out on the town feeling like a million dollars. Oliver Brown knew how to wear a suit, certainly but Nicky Starr…he'd been a connoisseur, a veritable fashion plate. Women and men had drooled over him and his fashion choices.

Oliver sighed in regret. Those days were over now, but still he kept to his tradition of ordering a new suit every month, sometimes more. He figured he had the money, heaps of it, sitting in the bank, so why not indulge in his collecting hobby?

"It's a new Debussy, I just had to have it…" his voice tailed off at the exasperated expletive on the other side of the phone.

"Ollie, honey, get your sexy ass down here right now or I might just have to disown you. I refuse to sit here looking like Lady Leftalone. I'll wait for you and order you a salad. That at least won't get cold while I sit here and twiddle my thumbs."

The phone clicked off and Oliver gazed at it and heaved another sigh. It was only ten minutes by tube to see Katie. Oliver enjoyed travelling the tubes where no one cared about each other, where it was all strangers with a complete disinterest for one's fellow man.

Sometimes when he was really lonely, Oliver would hop on one and travel as far as he could then come back again.

He huffed angrily at that reminder of just how pathetic he'd become and stalked through to the bedroom to change. He'd better get his arse into gear and make his way down to the little coffee place not too far away. It was quiet, secluded and the manager knew him well enough to know he didn't want any attention.

Oliver would hate to feel the wrong side of Katie's fist in his ribs. That woman packed a mean punch.

* * *

It was close to six p.m. when Oliver got home. He was both mentally and physically exhausted. He loved Katie, but she was hard work. They'd met on the set of one of his porn shoots; she'd been writing an article for a well-known lifestyle magazine on the relative difficulties of sustaining a true relationship given what the men involved did for a living. It had been a tasteful, sensitive article, highlighting the conflicts between separating the day job from the emotional and physical needs of having a lover, and had focused on the few monogamous relationships in the crew that Oliver had worked with.

Katie had been with him when he'd woken up, bleeding and broken in the hospital, in the aftermath of his coke-and-drink-fuelled orgy. She'd been his rock and his tormentor through the weeks and months that followed, refusing to give up on him.

Oliver poured himself a drink and sat down in the armchair overlooking the tatty garden. He got comfortable and draped his legs over the chair arm as he sat back at an angle, sipping his gin and tonic.

His iPad sat on the side table and he picked it up and idly flicked through his social networking sites. He used the name Justin Brown on most of them, Justin being his middle name, but kept his private details hidden and interacted only as much as he needed. It kept him in touch with the outside world to some small extent.

Oliver frowned when he saw a particular email in an inbox he monitored but had no reason to use any longer. It was on his old website, *www.nickystarr.co.uk*. The site was still active but he hadn't refreshed it in years. He still received a mountain of emails, mostly from men asking him if he was around either to fuck or be fucked. He ignored them all, but this one piqued his interest when he saw it was a Jacqui Lawson e-card sent by one Leslie Scott. Surely, it couldn't be the same man, could it? Curious, he opened it.

The card was called 'Monkey Business' and as Oliver watched, his lips curved in a smile. *This man is seriously goofy.* He was also cute as a button, plus stunningly beautiful. Oliver couldn't deny the warm feeling in his chest at the fact Leslie had actually taken the trouble to send him the card in the hope it would find him. When the little sketch with the organ grinder and the monkey had finished, the card read,

*I hope you get this. Your website is one of my most browsed. Sorry I was such an idiot. I really didn't mean to offend you so I hope you can forgive me if I said anything. Sometimes my mouth runs away with me.*

Oliver snorted with laughter, feeling cheerier than he had in a while. He didn't doubt the truth of *that* statement.

*I'd appreciate the chance to make it up to you. I'm giving you my mobile number and perhaps you'll call me and we can have coffee sometime. I'm not a stalker, promise.*

*Your # 1 Fan, Leslie Scott.*

*PS I pinkie swear that I only told my two BFFs about you. They won't talk. They know better. I honestly couldn't NOT tell them*

Another statement Oliver didn't doubt, even though it made him a little twitchy.

*PPS I hope you get a chance to wear the suit. I think you'd look awesome in it.*

A mobile number was listed at the end.

Glowing warmly inside, Oliver thought that maybe he might have made another friend. Someone who'd seen him at his worst and still wanted to be with him. He might just take Leslie up on his offer of coffee soon.

His old porn slogan, 'Get it On' flitted across his mind. Perhaps he'd do exactly that. The thought made him fall asleep with a soppy grin on his face.

# Chapter 5

"Leslie. There you are." Laverne's strident tones echoed in Leslie's ears. He stopped what he was doing, which was unpacking a recently arrived bale of silk into the storage cupboard, and smiled. He always welcomed an opportunity to speak with his boss.

"Morning, boss. And may I say you look stunning today? Very professional."

Dressed in a smart grey suit of her own design, with a ruffled white blouse and heels Leslie would kill for, Laverne grinned back with pale pink lips. "Well, thanks for noticing," she chirruped as she came to a halt before him. "I have a meeting with the bank today so I thought I'd better tone it down a bit." Laverne smiled wickedly. "I don't want to overshadow them with my more fabulous self when I'm asking them to give me money."

She grimaced as Leslie quickly finished arranging the bale *just so* on the shelf and closed the door. "I hate the bastards, watching their eyes glaze over when they see me then having to kow-tow to their officious arses. I suppose that's just the way of it."

Leslie nodded sagely. "My bank manager always insists on calling me Mr. Scott, which makes me feel like my dad and then proceeds to tell me yet again what an overdraft is made for." He sniffed. "Apparently it's not supposed to go over the limit all the time, and he gets quite agitated when I try to explain that that's what I thought it was *for*. Hence the word, *over*. I've no idea what the 'draft' thingie comes from though. That doesn't make any sense at all. I mean, that's something a writer does, like, with his first story, or when a cold wind blows through your door." Leslie shrugged.

Laverne chuckled, a deep, amused sound that made her broad shoulders shake. "Oh, I'd love to be a fly on the wall when you speak to your bank manager. You are too damn adorable."

Leslie grinned. "Maybe next time he phones me up with that apprehensive quiver in his voice, I should take you with me as my financial advisor. Now *that* would be a fun meeting."

Laverne rolled her eyes and snorted. "Leslie Scott, you are a demon incarnate. I wouldn't wish the two of us on any unsuspecting bank manager. Now, sweetie, I need a BIG favour from you." Her eyes glinted with mischief.

Leslie's gut roiled just a little.

"What do you need?" he asked cautiously, casting a furtive eye at the door in case someone was looking for him and he could be called away.

"Well, Dasher can't make it to the fashion show tomorrow night, some family emergency, so I need you to fill in for him." Laverne showed white teeth as she smiled.

Leslie's arse clenched in fear. "Oh hell, no. No way. Nuh-huh. Not me."

Dasher Godfrey was an icon in the fashion team, a man with nerves of steel and an unrelenting demeanour of tough, no-holds-barred attitude, who rousted all the models for the fashion shows and ensured they got on the catwalk on time and appropriately attired. It was a job he relished and everyone else dreaded. For him not to make it to an event, the family emergency had to be dire.

The models, male and female alike, with a few exceptions, it had to be said, were known in the company as *the spawn from hell*, and Leslie had no desire to be their next meal.

Laverne tut-tutted. "Now, Leslie, I know you can do it. Dasher isn't there but Bruce is, so all you'll really be doing is helping him herd the troops, do little jobs, stuff like that. Nothing too onerous."

The news that Bruce Mitchell, Dasher's part-time and very put-upon assistant, would be there was definitely a more palatable idea, but still Leslie demurred. "Laverne, you simply *cannot* ask that of me. I know nothing about getting the demons ready for the show, and hell, Dasher has an ulcer, is that what you want to do to me as well—"

A large, warm finger shut his flapping lips.

"Leslie, you can do it. And think of this as another thing to add to your CV. If you want to work in this industry, honey, you need to man up and grow a pair and face the terror that is the dressing room. It will be a wonderful experience for you." The finger was removed and Leslie opened his mouth to argue but Laverne waggled that finger in front of his face.

"No, no, no. It's a done deal. Tomorrow night, six p.m., at Mystique. I'll tell Brucie you're more than happy to help." With an airy wave and a waggle of her taut, muscled bottom, Laverne left the storeroom, no doubt prowling down the corridor to find another victim for a life-or-death favour.

Leslie scowled. "Crap and fuck," he muttered to himself as he picked up another bale of silk ready to pack away. "That's all I need." His face brightened as an idea came to him. "Maybe I can convince Taylor to come out tomorrow night with me and help. Eddie's had his turn to keep me company so I have a feeling Tay may be next to be subjected to the puppy-dog-eyed look. I did share my secret with him, after all."

Having met the infamous Nicky Starr, Leslie had been catapulted to almost superstardom in Eddie and Taylor's eyes. They enjoyed his films as much as Leslie and were keen to encourage him to pursue *Oliver Brown,* as it meant they might get to meet him, too. He'd made them pinkie swear not to tell anyone, including Gideon and Draven, even though he knew that was a lost cause. Eddie couldn't keep a secret. His freckled face was too expressive. But Leslie knew he could trust all four men to keep Oliver's situation under wraps.

Buoyed with his idea of having moral support and having backup for the event from hell tomorrow night, he finished packing the material and then went in search of sustenance in the form of Red Bull and a chicken Caesar salad.

* * *

"Kill me. Kill me now." Leslie's muttered growl was aimed at his rather limp BLT sandwich as he took the last savage bite out of it and threw away the empty wrapper. He glowered as he surveyed the maelstrom of activity that was the models' changing room. Beautiful men and women in various stages of undress assailed his weary eyes. His fingers were pricked bloody through various efforts to pin up fabric and tuck away bits that both the models and Laverne deemed unsuitable. He was bone tired, ratty and ready to go home.

He'd known he wasn't cut out for the constant pandering and sycophancy that went with keeping a fleet of highly paid divas in control, but this evening had been more than he could bear.

And that traitor Taylor, whom he'd thought would be sympathetic to his woes, was chatting up the naked man-hottie, a model called Reuben, on the other side of the room, and he was smiling and laughing as if he was born to be in a room with dicks, crotches, bums, tits and other unmentionables that Leslie wasn't prepared to name. Leslie wondered spitefully if his fiancé, Draven, knew about his lover's proclivity to flirt like a man-slut.

"Saying the forbidden name Voldemort has nothing on this," he muttered darkly. "There are lady bits everywhere…I can't even…" He shuddered. One of the models, Sasha, aimed a gimlet eye in his direction, and he closed his eyes, wishfully thinking if he couldn't see her, she wouldn't see him. It was a fruitless exercise. When he opened them, she stood in front of him, dressed only in a blue, sequinned thong which he might have fancied himself, her pert breasts only two inches from his face.

Leslie swallowed at having so much female flesh in close proximity. One of her manicured hands held out a stick of what looked like chalk.

"Rouge me," Sasha demanded and he stared at her blankly. From the corner of his eye he noticed Taylor glancing his way and moving toward him.

"Err, what?" Leslie said blankly.

Sasha clucked in impatience and stepped back a little. "Rub this," she held up the chalk, "On these." With her other hand, she indicated her breasts.

Leslie's jaw dropped wide open. Of all the things he'd had to do tonight, this had to be the worst.

"Why?" he said feebly. "I mean, you're going to be wearing something over them. A suit, aren't you? No one will see them…" His voice tailed off at the narrowed and angry eyes of the model.

"*I* will know," she imperiously. "It is a custom for me, and I want you to do it. Now. Put it on my nipples."

She forced the chalk into Leslie's hands and his gut churned. If Laverne hadn't been watching him with hawk eyes from the other side of the room, he'd have turned tail and run.

"I'd suggest you get to it, Leslie." Taylor's barely contained chuckle at his side caused Leslie to glower darkly at his friend. "I mean, you don't want to mess with Sasha's traditions, do you? That's bad luck." He snorted loudly.

"Fuck you," Leslie mouthed at him. Taylor bent over in laughter.

"*Da.*" Sasha nodded fiercely, her eyes conveying her approval of Taylor's words. "Bad luck not to do it." She thrust her chest and dusky nipples out toward Leslie. He gave a heart-wrenching sigh of resignation and with shaking hands, raised the reddish chalk towards the pinnacles of female perfection. Wincing, he circled one with the chalk, once, twice then did the same to the other. The nipples now stood out darkly against Sasha's tanned skin and she stared at them critically. Then she bestowed a dazzling smile on Leslie and leaned forward to kiss him on the forehead.

"*Spaseeba*," she squealed, turned and disappeared with a flourish of tanned, very firm arse. Leslie levelled his fiery gaze at Taylor who was struggling to keep his composure.

"You are such a prick," he said evenly as Taylor gasped in amusement.

"I have one of those, yes," Taylor spluttered. "Oh God, Leslie, your face. It was too damn precious. You looked as if someone had asked you to eat a baby."

"That might have been preferable," Leslie muttered. "Honestly, what else are these people going to expect me to do tonight?"

His question was answered sooner than he'd anticipated. Another of the models, Bernsen Jenner, sauntered over, all one hundred and fifty pounds of him, stark naked, with a dick that looked as if it could be used as a third leg to kick start a jumbo jet.

Bernsen waved toward his crotch. Leslie stared and he noticed Taylor was having a good look, too.

"Leslie, my dumpling," he crooned. "I need you to trim some stray hairs for me. My B is looking a little untidy."

Leslie shook his head in disbelief at the vision that was Bernsen's crotch. His groin was artfully shaved with the initials B and J either side of the meaty appendage that swung between his legs. This was still better than dealing with lady parts, and Leslie was quick to nod his head. After all, dicks and balls were more his speciality.

"Sure," he burbled, "Glad to." He reached over to a nearby dressing table and grabbed a pair of clippers.

"More your thing, then," whispered Taylor in his ear as he continued staring at Bernsen's dick. "I'm really glad you invited me tonight. This has been an awesome evening."

"Uh huh," Leslie said as he knelt down before Bernsen, feeling uncomfortably as if he was about to give a blow job. "Wait until I tell Draven how much you enjoyed yourself."

He revelled in the sight of Taylor's discomfort at that veiled threat as he worked. Bernsen gave a mournful sigh as he watched

Leslie busy himself tidying up the man's bush, pushing his dick away gently to one side.

"You pay two hundred pounds for a manscape and this is what you get," the model fretted. "There is no sense of service anymore. Everyone is just out for a fast buck."

Leslie nodded. "Well, I manscape, too. Sometimes I do it myself and sometimes I go to the salon. And it looks nothing like *this*." He narrowed his eyes as he snipped stray hairs. "Is this one of your pre-show customs then, Bernsen?"

The model gave him a sly look from under perfectly manicured eyebrows. "Custom? No, my plum, I just think you are too adorable and I like your hands on my body."

Leslie blushed pink in pleasure. He finished up and stood back to admire his handiwork. In truth, he thought that there was little difference, but he'd tried to make Bernsen happy.

The model looked down and inspected his groin. "Looks better. Thank you, my sweetheart." He patted Leslie's head and turned and disappeared into the throng that milled around.

Leslie chuckled. "I love the whole BJ thing. I wonder if he gets much action with that design. Do you think he just drops his pants and pushes his crotch out at someone and he gets an instant blow job?"

Taylor flapped a hand. "I'm still in shock finding out how much he paid for the damn shave. I'd have done it for him at half the price. The shave, not the BJ. Although…" He leered and Leslie pursed his lips.

"You, my friend, are a complete tart." He grinned. "That makes two of us. I still wouldn't have paid that much though for a treatment."

Just then, Camilla, one of the models currently standing around, waiting to be dressed, gave a loud unladylike snort. She put her thumbs in her barely there, canary yellow thong and pulled them down. "Huh. What do you think *this* is?' She indicated her crotch and stared at him.

Leslie wasn't really sure what she was asking or pointing to. There was so much bronzed and pink-lipped flesh on display he felt a little nauseous.

"Uhmm, a vagina?" he proffered weakly.

The model gave him a withering glance. "Darling, you are definitely *so* gay if you think a woman's vagina is on the outside of her body."

Leslie's face heated up at the sniggers around him—Taylor's the loudest. "I know where a woman's vagina is," he said haughtily. "But honestly, I wasn't sure what you were pointing to." He swallowed. "It was rather open to interpretation, really."

Taylor's chuckles grew louder and Leslie turned to glare at his amused friend. Bruce had joined them and was watching the proceedings with laughter on his face.

Camilla's hand waved at her crotch. "This, my clueless friend, is a *three* hundred-pound wax job. We all pay a lot to look as good as we do. So I don't think your Bic razor job comes close." She sniffed and stalked off as Leslie watched her, open-mouthed.

"Bitch," he sniffed. "I don't use a Bic."

Taylor exploded in laughter, his face pink. Despite himself, a smile tugged at Leslie's lips. "Bastards," he said affably at Taylor. "If you were forced to stare at women's bits, I'd bet you'd sing a different tune." He cast a glance at Bruce. "Except you, old man, because everyone knows you *love* the ladies…"

Bruce guffawed. "Working around this lot of divas is enough to put you off 'em for life," he snorted. "But I do admit this job has its perks."

\* \* \*

An hour later Leslie was sitting in a small storage cupboard, surrounded by various old props, clothing, towels and smelly laundry. He'd had enough of everyone, so he'd slunk away to check his emails and texts for the first time that day. His overriding hope was that Oliver had responded to his cute monkey card. Leslie had known it was a long shot but he lived forever in hope. He made himself comfortable on a pile of old towels, stretched his legs out before him and heaved a sigh of relief as he pulled out his smartphone. No one would think to look for him in here.

He wrinkled his nose in distaste at the reek in the room. "Smells freaky," he grumbled to himself. "But at least it's private and I can think."

He flicked quickly through his messages and his heart skipped a beat when he got to his texts. In fact, Leslie was sure he squealed like a *Supernatural* fan meeting Dean up close and personal. "He texted me!"

Hands trembling with excitement, he opened the message.

*Hi Leslie. Got yr card. Tks, it was rly cool. Hope u r well. Coffee sounds gd. Oliver.*

Leslie sat back against the wall and took a deep breath. "Oh hell. He wants to go for coffee." He texted back quickly.

*OMG, gd to hear from u. Glad u lkd card. When do u wnt to meet up?*

His eyes watched the small screen, willing a reply. After about ten minutes had elapsed, he sighed.

*He's probably not got his phone on him.*

Leslie kept telling himself that even after the day from hell ended. Taylor had been philosophical about the fact Oliver had texted him, but not called back yet.

"Give him some time," he'd advised, a twinkle in his eye. "He might have lost signal or something. Maybe give it a day or so, see if he gets back to you."

\* \* \*

Now Leslie was home in his small, minimally decorated apartment, curled up on the couch with his favourite fuzzy socks on and a warm tracksuit. He wouldn't been seen dead in what he called his *sloth clothes* in public, but at home, on his own, he rather enjoyed the freedom to be a slob. It was hard work looking as good he did all the time.

He fed his fish, added an extra castle he'd bought to the fish tank so Glenda, a small clown fish, could try something new—the fish seemed to have a thing for hiding behind castles—then made himself a cup of hot chocolate.

He watched the news on television with eyes that barely took it in and kept darting to his phone every five minutes. When the phone finally rung and he was dozing on the large red throw pillow, he sat up with a start. The strident tones of Lady Gaga's 'Born This Way' echoed in the stillness of his lounge and he scrambled dozily for his mobile. It was an unknown caller and for a moment, Leslie was tempted not to answer. He'd been the subject of harassment before from a guy he'd given his number to and now he was a little wary. The thought in his head though that this could be Oliver calling made him waive his natural tendency to ignore the insistent ringing and he answered.

"This is Leslie." He mentally crossed his fingers hoping psycho stalker Brian hadn't managed to track him down.

"Leslie?" The hesitant voice on the other side made Leslie want to squee in delight.

*It was him.*

"Oliver?"

"Uhmm, yes. You recognise my voice then?" He sounded amused and Leslie's heart beat faster.

"Of course. It's only been a couple of weeks since I saw you. My memory isn't that bad."

"Yeah, I'm sorry it took so long to reply to you. I was…busy." There was a short silence. "I thought we could meet up somewhere on Thursday evening. You know, just for a chat and a cup of coffee." His voice was hesitant but firm.

Leslie pursed his lips.

*Ah, setting the expectations. He sounds a little skittish. I can be his friend if that's all he wants. I don't want to scare him off. I know I can be a bit…intense.*

"I'd like that; coffee sounds good. If you text me the address where you want to meet, I can meet you there after work on Thursday."

"Uh, sure. It's a little place called Fidalgo's, not far from my house. I'll text you the details. The owner knows me, so just mention my name when you get there and he'll show you through."

Leslie nodded happily. "That sounds good. I look forward to it."

Oliver sounded more relaxed when next he spoke. "Yeah, me, too. It'll be good to chat to you. I'll see you then."

The phone went silent and Leslie did a little jig around the lounge. He saw Mrs. Camberwell from across the courtyard in the opposite block of flats watching him from her window.

He pranced over to the large picture window and waved. "Hi, Mrs C. I've got a coffee date with a porn star—well, ex porn star." He knew she couldn't hear him but she waved back and disappeared.

Ever since he'd danced naked in front of the window one evening and she'd seen him, she'd been very friendly. He'd been rather drunk at the time, he had to admit. Luckily she hadn't seen the sexual calisthenics that had occurred after Leslie's date had pulled him back from his exhibition of Michael Flatley's *Riverdance* routine and pushed him onto his knees on the carpet. The guy—Darren, Darryl?—had had the presence of mind to close the curtains before fucking him senseless.

That image brought back some fond memories. After sending a message to both Taylor and Eddie with the joyful news Oliver had called him back, Leslie used that memory to jack off later to the face of Nicky Starr in his heyday, blissfully content that on Thursday, he'd get to meet the real man behind the mystery.

## Chapter 6

Oliver sat at his usual table at Fidalgo's, his fingers nervously tapping the red-chequered table top. His stomach was in knots and he'd barely slept last night. He'd even thought of crying off today and telling Leslie that something had come up and he wouldn't make it. However, the thought of Katie—who'd highly approved of the coffee plan—bitching at him for *not* going was worse than the alternative.

And he really did want to see Leslie again. He'd thought of nothing more from their last phone call. It would be good to talk someone who was so bright and bubbly and, he admitted to himself, sex on a stick. Although that wasn't what he wanted from this, he reminded himself. He needed a friend, not a lover. And besides, he doubted Leslie would be interested in him that way. He probably had a string of undamaged goods at his beck and call.

*For God's sake, stop analysing everything and get on with it.*

Despite that thought, his cock throbbed in his black jeans when he saw Leslie enter the coffee shop. The man looked like he had just stepped out of a fashion magazine. Dressed in tight black chinos, finished with high-heeled black boots, with a white collared shirt and a leather jacket, wearing the biggest pair of sunglasses Oliver had ever seen, Leslie looked mouth-wateringly tempting. His jet black hair was styled artfully over his face, one strand of hair falling down, making Oliver want to brush it away. He took Oliver's breath away.

*Down boy*, he cautioned himself. *Keep it simple. Just friends, remember?*

Alberto, the owner, approached Leslie and gestured, then his coffee date looked over to where Oliver sat and the most beautiful smile flooded his face.

*Oh dear God*, Oliver thought desperately. *I am in so much fucking trouble.*

He didn't dare stand up for fear the hard-on he sported would spring free in celebration of Leslie's presence. Instead he remained seated, uncomfortably so, and as Leslie approached the table, he waved at the chair opposite, willing his erection to go down with thoughts of copulating old men with hairy bodies and limp dicks.

"Leslie. Glad you could make it."

Leslie seated himself at the table and flashed another grin. "I like this place. Very trendy. And that guy on the front desk is yummy." His blue eyes cast a mischievous glance toward Enrico, one of Alberto's sons who'd just arrived at the reception stand. Enrico looked down at the desk, a smile on his face. A sudden rush of jealousy assailed Oliver.

*Where the hell did that come from?*

He quashed the unreasonable emotion and waved toward one of the passing waiters. "What kind of coffee would you like?"

"Oh, just a plain latte for me. I'm not one of those 'caramel macchiato, venti, skim, extra shot, sugar free, no foam, extra hot' crazy people."

Oliver blinked. "That's a drink?"

Leslie huffed. "Oh my God, yes. Before I got this job at Debussy, I worked at Starbucks. You cannot believe the fussiness of some people out there with their coffee orders. I needed a dictionary sometimes to look up some of the words they used."

Drinks ordered, they settled into chat about the recent week. Leslie's hilarious account of his evening at the fashion event, including the side-splitting nipple-rouging, made Oliver laugh as he hadn't in years. Leslie's dry, sarcastic account of his escapades was delivered in a voice that Oliver thought could melt hearts, and his facial expressions and hand gestures were classic. His sides were aching when Leslie finished his story and threw him another dazzling smile.

"So that's my week. What have you been doing with yourself then?" His eyes slid appraisingly down Oliver's body. Oliver's dick took notice.

"I have to say, that colour green really suits you." Leslie murmured. "That shirt brings out the colour of your eyes and the cut is really flattering. But then what would you expect from a Ralph Lauren?" He shrugged slim shoulders as he removed his sunglasses and tucked them into his man bag.

Oliver had spent close to two hours debating what to wear and the fact he'd chosen well made his body glow. "It's an old favourite. Team it with comfortable jeans and it's a no-brainer for a coffee date."

Leslie's eyes met his and Oliver's hand moved unconsciously to his hair as he made sure it covered his scar.

"You look perfect," Leslie said softly. "Honestly, stop worrying about it."

"It's a habit," Oliver muttered. "Especially when I'm out in public." His hand strayed to his hair again and he took a deep breath when Leslie reached across and stayed his nervous movement. Leslie's touch ignited something in his heart and his groin.

"I'm not the public." Leslie said softly. "I'm just someone hoping to be your friend."

Oliver nodded then moved his hands away from his hair and picked up his coffee. Leslie unnerved him like no one in a long, long time. "I think that can be arranged." He grinned and the awkward moment passed.

An hour later there was a lull in the conversation as Enrico bought them another cup of coffee. Oliver frowned. Enrico didn't normally do table duty. In fact, he hated being a waiter, considering it beneath him as the owner's son. Oliver scowled as Leslie flirted and their waiter's normally monosyllabic responses got chattier. Oliver's ire grew even worse when he pressed a business card into Leslie's hand with the whisper to 'call me.'

"That guy is a prick," Oliver growled when Enrico was out of earshot. "I don't want to interfere in your love life, but you should know that."

Leslie's eyes widened innocently. "But he's so darned cute." He laughed as Oliver growled again and drained his coffee cup. "I tell you what, let's forget about the hot Italian stud over there and tell me more about yourself. I'm dying to know what you've been doing the last couple of years, being out of the industry. What do you do for a living? Do you have a job?"

Oliver nodded. "I do web design. Mostly, I get referrals and build customised sites for people. It's a good living and I'm lucky—I have rather a captive clientele." He cleared his throat. "I build a lot of adult sites, sex aid sites, some BDSM ones, that sort of thing."

Leslie's eyes got bigger. "Oh my God, really? How cool. Give me some examples; let's see if I know any of them."

Oliver leaned back in his chair. "Well, I built Leo's new site, Leo Loving, but that wasn't porn. It was his new film studio site. Then there was Donny Dickson, Jerry Jarvis and that new guy, Luke Lecher." He grimaced at Leslie's snort. "I know, terrible name. What's with these guys and all the alliteration? But the guy threw a lot of money at me to create his website so I tried to give him what he wanted."

Oliver was enjoying himself. He didn't really get to talk about his current work much. He warmed to his subject. "There's something about sitting in front of a computer and listening to what a client wants, then trying to put it all together. It's pretty creative, actually, to try and be different, when everyone thinks a porn site is all about hot bods and fucking. Of course that's the main thing, but there's also the merchandising aspect, the advertising revenues, the ability to let your fans interact with you too, and share their fantasies. It's about creating something special where people can lose themselves. I created the Nicky Starr site myself and let me tell you, it's damned hard work." He stopped at the look of merriment on Leslie's face. "What?"

"God, you are such a geek. It's adorable." Leslie's blue eyes twinkled with mirth.

Oliver flushed. He *had* been rambling a bit. "Sorry, I get carried away sometimes."

"I love it," Leslie purred. "It's a bit like me when I talk fashion and fabrics. Then all anyone wants to do is stuff something in my mouth to make me shut up."

And didn't *that* thought make Oliver harder than a stick of dynamite. His expression must have communicated his thoughts because Leslie's pale face pinked up.

"Oh, wait, I didn't mean it *that* way…"

Oliver couldn't help himself. He burst out laughing and soon Leslie had joined in and they were both chortling like school kids. Enrico cast them a dirty glance—Oliver thought it might have been directed at him.

When the dirty thoughts stopped circling his brain at just how much he'd like to shut Leslie up, Oliver wiped his eyes.

"Hell. That just tickled me." For one brief moment, he forgot his scar and tucked the hair that hung down his face behind his right ear. No sooner had he realised what he'd done, than he flicked it back again in panic, covering it up.

Leslie leant forward and ran a warm finger down his jawline, taking care not to touch the jagged scar. Oliver hadn't had anyone touch that side of his face in years. His heart and body thrummed with need and yearning.

"Maybe one day you'll tell me exactly how you got that." Leslie moved his hand away as Oliver swallowed and then looked down at the table. A long moment later, he looked up into Leslie's cerulean eyes. They were warm and there was no pity in them.

*I can do this.*

He took a deep breath. "I was twenty-three and I thought I was immortal. Untouchable. It was the height of my career and I had everything a man could want. A career, more money than I knew what to do with and a radical motorbike." His lips twisted in a smile. "His name was Hulk and he was huge and green just like Bruce Banner when he turned. I'd been to a party and got shit-faced on coke." He stopped, his throat dry. "I was pretty addicted to the stuff. It helped me cope with the demands of performing and the pressure to be *someone* constantly." He didn't want to get into the reason for him being at that party that night and getting out of control. That was a story for another time.

Leslie's calm face watched him without judgement. The only trace of emotion in his face was the slight tic in his jaw.

"That night all the guys wanted to check out the porn star, see how good he was. I ended up screwing about three or four of them. I needed some encouragement so I was as high as a bloody kite. Coke and booze. Then I got on Hulk to race one of them. It was a macho display that everyone knew wouldn't end well. But I didn't listen." He closed his eyes as the memories flooded back. "I hit a bend, slid and then hit the side of the road. It was pretty rocky and I went flying, straight over a barbed wire fence and into a field. The thing was, there was a load of scrap metal in a pile in the middle of the grass and it ripped my face and my right arm wide open, as well as the side of my body."

Leslie made a small sound of horror and reached over to take Oliver's hand in his. Oliver curled his large fingers around Leslie's fine-boned ones. The touch of the other man grounded him and he carried on.

"I broke some ribs, my left arm and a couple of my fingers. I had a ruptured spleen and as well as the side of my face being damaged, it affected my eye. Tore the muscle which is why it droops slightly. My right arm was virtually ripped open from wrist to shoulder and I have bad scarring along it, along with a bit of muscle loss. But physical therapy helped me get it back to almost normal. It just aches sometimes and I can't pick up anything too heavy."

"Oh my God." Leslie's face was white and Oliver saw his eyes glistening. "I'm so glad you made it out alive. I mean, it could have been much worse."

Oliver sighed tiredly. "I was very lucky to avoid blood poisoning afterward. The emergency services were quick to get me to hospital, and I had the best medical care money could buy. My film studio, Vanguard, went all out on that one." He tightened his fingers around Leslie's.

"I spent a long time in hospital, having plastic surgery and skin grafts for it all." His memories of the pain and frustration he'd suffered through too many surgical procedures made his stomach lurch. "And this…" he motioned toward his face, "was the end result." He gave a twisted smile. "As well as some other nice scars."

*Rounded off by having my lover of a year walk out because he couldn't stand the sight of me. And getting over a cocaine addiction.*

"Where was your family?" Leslie asked. "Didn't your parents help you though this?"

Oliver shook his head ruefully. "My folks live in Australia. Dad works a low-paid job and Mum is a housewife. They still don't know about my time in the porn industry. I didn't want them ever knowing either, so I didn't tell them about the accident until after it was all over and I was much better. They had no money to come out here. It would have bankrupted them and they may have found out what their son was doing." He gave a tired laugh. "I just told them I'd had a fall off the bike but never told them how bad it was. I haven't seen them face-to-face in years. We Skype now and then and I make sure they can't see my face properly."

"God, that's so sad, having to lie to your folks like that. My folks live in Scotland with my older brother, Nathan. I see them now and then." Leslie managed a wistful smile. "I think you look a lot like Jon Bon Jovi with that shaggy-hair look. He's damn hot; well, he was when he had that hair style. And I rather like the metrosexual bearded look."

"Thank you," Oliver said softly. "I don't get too many compliments anymore on how I look."

Leslie's eyes narrowed and he leaned forward, pursing soft lips that Oliver really wanted to kiss. "That, my friend, is because you don't get out much. It's your own damn fault for hiding away in that house with only a wardrobe of suits to keep you company." He grinned and Oliver's insides melted. "I know about your love of them, of course. I've seen your website. Plus I looked back at your purchases. You, my friend, have a problem. You must have bought about twenty suits from Debussy's over the past couple of years." He made a moue. "Not that it's a problem. Keeps me in a job buying that fabric you love so Laverne can make your suits. She loves you, by the way. You're her best customer."

Oliver chuckled. "No doubt she does. Her designs just have this appeal for me; they're so classic and sexy. I can't help myself."

Leslie cluck clucked. "Then we need to get you out and about in them more. Show you off."

Oliver shook his head, his heart heavy. "Not going to happen, Leslie. I go out only when I have to. Otherwise I'm fine by myself. I've managed so far."

Leslie's eyes softened. "I didn't mean get you out in the middle of a film premiere with 101 cameras sighted on you, doofus. I meant perhaps going to a great dinner in an intimate restaurant where I know the owner will protect your privacy and chase away anyone that bothers you. Gideon can be pretty scary when he wants to be."

Oliver had to say the idea tempted him, both getting into a new suit to go out and spending more time with Leslie. He nodded hesitantly. "Maybe we can do that." His heart beat a little faster. "Are you asking me out on a date, Leslie?"

Leslie looked taken aback then shook his head. "No, as one friend to another. Now that my two housemates have both moved in with the men of their dreams, I'm no longer part of a threesome. I miss having someone to hang out with."

Oliver raised an eyebrow. He couldn't deny he was a little disappointed at Leslie's response this wasn't a date. "A threesome? Are you into ménage then?" It was something he'd been involved in many times in his porn career and perhaps a few times after he retired. He was taken aback by his coffee partner's vehement response.

"Hell, no. I'm not into that sort of thing." Leslie's beautiful face contorted in a frown. "I know you are, but to tell you the truth, they weren't my favourite scenes of you. I prefer my actions man-on-man, not men-on-men."

"Oh." Oliver was nonplussed. "There's a lot of that in the industry. Sometimes I had to do the scenes, and they were fun, but not a personal preference." He shrugged.

"I want a relationship, not a fuck-fest," Leslie muttered. "Some of the guys I went out with in the past, all they wanted me for was to be the meat in the middle of a man sandwich and sometimes I had to think quickly to get out of being the hole in a full on gang bang."

Oliver gaped as the rising fury in his chest surfaced. "Did they try and force you? Did anyone hurt you? I swear I'll fuck them up—"

Leslie's face lit up and he laughed as he placed a warm hand on Oliver's. "Oh God, that is so damn sweet. My protector. No, sometimes it got a bit hairy balls and I had to make a swift exit, but I was always careful." His face fell. "Well, apart from this one time I already mentioned, when a friend saved me from a fate worse than death because he can see things. He knew I was in trouble and came to find me." He smiled wryly, holding up his thumb and index finger only slightly apart. "I was this close to being mauled by a couple of guys who I still think slipped me something in my drink, but my friend Taylor found me. He's a psychic."

That offhand comment left Oliver curious. "Really? A real one?" He'd never met someone with that particular talent before.

Leslie nodded, eyes sparkling. "Oh, yeah. He saved Eddie's cousin Luke when he tried to kill himself, and he helped solve a suicide, and he even helped Draven's little brother move onto the other side when he managed to contact him somewhere." He flapped a vague hand. "Somewhere in between here and heaven I suppose, and Draven turned off Jude's life support and we all hope he's gone somewhere really cool to be with his parents. They're dead, too."

Oliver was reeling from all the names and information thrown at him in this rather surreal conversation.

"Taylor is amazing," Leslie sighed, a faraway look in his eyes. "My bestest friend, really. I love Eddie, but Taylor and I, we just click together. He's awesome."

Oliver was beginning to take a distinct dislike to the paragon of virtue who was Taylor. "Are you and he, you know, partners?"

Leslie broke into peals of laughter. "Oh no, we'd kill each other. We've jerked each other off now and then and shared a bed a few times, but that's about it. God, Draven would kill me if I touched

Taylor. " He winked at a slightly mollified Oliver. "And you don't want to get on Draven's bad side. He can be a real grouch and he has wicked self-defence skills and boy, can that man drive a car."

Oliver began to wonder if he was man enough for all these super hero he-men characters that Leslie seemed to know.

"So what does Eddie do then?" he asked snarkily. "Toss dwarves, fight rabid wolves, maybe slay a dragon or two?"

Leslie collapsed into snorts of laughter then raised a hand to his mouth. "Sorry, you got me snorting again. You're the only man who can do that, I swear." Oliver was gratified that there was something he could do that the Marvellous Avengers couldn't. "Nope, Eddie is a chef. An award-winning one. He just won the London Chef of the Year award a couple of weeks ago. "

Oliver wanted to roll his eyes, but that would have been rude. Now he had to contend with super chefs as well. He couldn't help feeling a little put out. "Oh, well, that's cool I suppose. I—"

Leslie nodded eagerly as he butted in. "He's one of the chefs at the restaurant I want to take you to. Eddie's boyfriend, Gideon, he owns Galileo's in Soho. He's a chef, too, only he's just starting to cook again because he got burned in a fire and lost a couple of his senses. Now that he's starting to get his smell and taste buds back, he's returned to the kitchen again. You'll enjoy meeting them, and Galileo's is like, the best place ever." He stopped to take a breath and Oliver saw his chance to actually participate in the conversation.

"Okay, that sounds like a plan. I can meet these two friends of yours and try out one of my suits and get a good meal, too. Win-win situation, I'd say. Any idea when you want to do this da—this dinner?"

Leslie pulled out his really fancy phone and flicked through it, muttering to himself. Oliver sighed. He should have known a guy like Leslie had a heavy social calendar and probably had to book his events weeks or months in advance. He was about to tell Leslie that it was fine and to forget dinner if he was that busy when Leslie waved his phone at him and beamed brightly.

"How about next Friday, the thirtieth? That's only eight days away." His face fell. "I'd like it to be sooner, but this weekend I'm working at a fashion show, helping them out with the setup and organising, and Laverne will have my balls if I cancel. Plus, I could use the overtime money she's paying me."

It seemed a bit far away, but Oliver tamped down his disappointment at having to wait over a week to see Leslie again.

"Sure," he agreed nonchalantly. "It's not like I have many other plans. Except, maybe drinks with my friend Katie. You'll have to meet her. I think the two of you will get along really well. She's crazy, too." He flashed a grin at Leslie who grinned back.

"I'd love to meet her, just as long as she isn't one of those women who insist on telling me all about her girly bits. I get enough of that at work, thank you very much."

"I think I can safely say that's not something you have to worry about."

Oliver was truly gutted when the afternoon came to an end. He stood up as Leslie collected his belongings, which had been strewn across the table like debris from a rock fall and stuffed everything into his fancy man-bag. For a moment, the two men looked at each other awkwardly. Finally Leslie stepped up and placed a soft kiss on Oliver's undamaged cheek and hugged him tightly.

"Thanks for this afternoon. I really enjoyed it. I'll text you the details of where to find Galileo's, unless you'd like me to pick you up? I can always borrow the work car."

Oliver shook his head. "No, it's fine, I'll tube it. I quite like the trains. All anonymous and no one really cares who you are."

Leslie nodded. "Okay. Well, I look forward to next Friday then. Enjoy your weekend. Tell your friend Katie I say hi." He slung his bag across his shoulder and with one last wave, he turned and walked away.

Oliver watched him go with mixed feelings. One part of him wanted to grab the man and take him home and pound the hell out of him. The other, a warm fuzzy feeling, told him he'd just made a friend and not to fuck it up.

He sighed as he put on his jacket. Oh well, he had Friday next week to look forward to. In the meantime, he'd use the image of Leslie's pert arse as his masturbation material for the coming week. He might even give Maxwell a call, see if his friend was in town. Maybe getting laid would rid him of this ache he had inside, the dread that coiled persistently in his stomach. It had been with him as long as he could remember.

Sex would help him forget, let him enter the zone where he could switch off and just enjoy the physical exertion. Yes, he'd definitely be giving Max a call.

## Chapter 7

In bed that night, Leslie lay on top of the covers, clad in his favourite pair of red satin boxers and a pair of matching Christian Louboutin heels. His hand was inside his underwear and wrapped firmly around his dick. He loved the feeling of silk on his hands as he jerked off. It also made clean up less messy, although the laundry bill took a beating.

The room was warm and cosy, with just the dim bedside light highlighting the activity on the TV screen. Leslie watched from beneath half-closed eyes as Nicky Starr disrobed slowly, stripping off the suit he wore bit by bit until only his shirt and tie remained, the tie loose and strung around his neck like that of a naughty schoolboy flouting authority. Nicky's hard and rather pleasing cock jutted upward and Leslie imagined taking it in his mouth, licking it from root to tip, then swallowing it whole. The thought raised goose pimples on his skin, and he could almost taste the man in his mouth, the rich scent that Nicky would exude on his tongue, and smell the man's cologne in his nostrils. Oliver had been wearing Hugo Boss and the smell of it still lingered in Leslie's imagination.

"Oh God, yes," he whispered huskily as he stroked his lubed cock, and his body embraced the rising pleasure that was unfolding. He opened his legs wider, planting his stiletto heels deeper into the bed cover. "God, Leo is so damn lucky." He watched Nicky move onto the bed like a panther, still half dressed as he loomed over the waiting man on the bed. This film, a nautical-themed dalliance called *Scent of Semen* was one of Leslie's all-time favourite Nicky Starr and Leo Loving performances. The two men had on-screen chemistry and Leo's slim, lithe frame currently writhed in pleasure on the bed as Nicky lowered his head and took him deep into his mouth. Leslie imagined those lips around his own cock, sucking and licking and teasing and he twisted on the bed as his hands grew firmer on his dick. The action on screen got intense as Leo turned over and got on his hands and knees then sank down to the bed on his elbows and looked back at Nicky with a cheeky grin.

"Go on," he murmured, "Eat me out. I know you want to. Want to feel your tongue in my hole, stretching me, then your beautiful cock inside me, making me scream. Fuck me, Captain."

Nicky growled, a sound that struck the nerve endings in Leslie's body, and he panted slowly as he watched Nicky lower his mouth to Leo's arse. What followed nearly made him cream himself but he wanted to hold out just that little longer, feel himself come as Nicky's tongue pushed his way fiercely into Leo, imagine that was *him* on the bed and Oliver behind him. The image he had on his screen might have been Nicky Starr, porn star, but it was Oliver, beautiful damaged Oliver, who Leslie had in his mind right now. Oliver, whom he wanted to do that to him, Oliver who would finally push inside him and make Leslie cry out in pleasure as he came.

The noises on screen got louder as Nicky finally lubed Leo up enough to grab his hips and ram inside him. The sight of that perfect cock disappearing inside Leo and Leo's strangled cry of pleasure was enough to make Leslie frantically jack himself off harder, all the while imagining that cock inside *him*, until he came, hard, with a shuddering of limbs, a heaving of breath and a spurt of semen that looked as if it was trying out for the National Semen Javelin Championships. Unfortunately that powerful orgasm hadn't contained itself to his satin boxers. His belly was sticky and his treasure trail matted with come.

"Oh my fucking God," Leslie panted as his body shivered and jerked on the bed, his semi-hard dick still clutched in his hands. "That was awesome." The pleasure suffusing his post-orgasmic body was buoyed by the knowledge he'd actually had coffee with the man on screen today and that in just over a week's time, he'd be seeing him again. And yes, Leslie knew he was trying to be friends with Oliver first but he was also honest enough to admit that he wanted the man to fuck him just like Leo had been. He wanted Oliver here, in his bed, to cuddle and wake up to, wanted the warmth of that hard body next to his, smiling sleepily at him in the morning.

And one way or another, Leslie Tiberius Scott was going to get that wish.

\* \* \*

Oliver was horny. Fed up that Maxwell had been out of the country—again—and he was left to his own devices, he'd already jerked off in the shower soon after leaving Leslie today. The relief had been short lived. He'd finished washing, wrapped a towel around his waist and as he'd gone to put his shirt into the laundry, he'd caught a whiff of Leslie's scent. It was some warm, spicy fragrance that had him sniffing deeply at the sweaty shirt, and getting hard again as he imagined those soft lips on his cheek and the taut litheness of Leslie's body against his as he'd hugged him goodbye.

Now, with a groan, he shoved the shirt into his wicker laundry basket and put the towel back on the rail. He padded naked over to his DVD collection and opened the door to one of the cupboards. Eyes quickly perused the contents; he soon found what he was looking for. It was one of his own performances, one he'd done with a cute guy called Adam, who bore a remarkable resemblance to Leslie. Oliver remembered him fondly. Adam had been all black hair and soft chuckles, with a body that had been sublime and the way he used it even better. Oliver had never been ridden like that before in his life, and truth be told, Adam had the knack of making a man feel like a prime stallion. Especially when he'd worn his heels, something Oliver was partial to in a man.

With a sense of anticipation, he put the DVD into his player and got comfortable on the couch. For these sessions, he tended to put down a towel first to keep the couch clean from sticky fluids. Even though he didn't get many visitors, Oliver was house proud. Dried semen on the seats tended to be off-putting to guests.

The film, titled *The War Whore*, started and Oliver wondered if he was a narcissist watching his own movie. However, he wanted to see Adam in action, imagine it was Leslie above him, see those cobalt blue eyes staring into his as he fucked him. His cock rose and Oliver sighed in satisfaction as his hands got busy. There was something to be said about living alone and having the privacy to jack off in your own living room using the lube that was scattered around the place.

Through lazy eyes, he watched himself lying on a medieval divan, dressed in an opened leather waistcoat, chest hair showing. He remembered that those pants had been the most uncomfortable leather ones he'd ever worn. They were opened to show his cock upright and purpled, already glistening and definitely ready for the slave who stood in front of him. Adam smiled invitingly on screen and dropped his tunic to reveal an impressive dick and a slim, muscled body. He also had a backside that you could bounce coins off. The man's arse had been bite-worthy, and Oliver's mouth filled with saliva as he imagined what Leslie's would be like. From what he'd seen today, the man had a tight, bubble arse and Oliver really wanted in.

Languid strokes to his cock made his pulse race; his mouth opened and his heavy breaths echoed in the room. He watched the events playing out on screen, as Adam straddled him and then rammed down on his cock with a fierce battle cry and began to bounce up and down like a yo-yo. Oliver closed his eyes and imagined that scene, but with Leslie in the slave role. Black bangs over blue eyes framed a face that was pale and delicate, yet with the strength of a man's jaw and square cheekbones that made no mistake about the gender of the person currently riding Oliver's cock.

He opened his eyes as his hands tightened around his dick, and the lube and his own fluids slicked him and sent waves of pleasure down to his feet, his arse and pooled in his groin.

"Oh, God, Leslie," he gasped, as he watched Adam rise and fall against Nicky's thrusting hips and heard the sounds of pleasure as Nicky Starr pushed deep inside the slave. "I want you so damn badly…" His voice caught as the pressure in his groin grew relentless and he cried out as he climaxed, come jettisoning across his stomach in white streams, the sheer volume leaving Oliver feeling empty and drained. He hadn't realised how tense he'd been and he slumped back against the couch arm, waves of lethargy washing over him as he relaxed.

Thank God for the towel, he thought drowsily as he closed his eyes, pulled a blanket he kept close over him and imagined Leslie lying next to him, curled up against his side like a sleepy kitten. He'd love to have the warmth of a man's body next to him, hear the slight exhalations as he slept, wake up to the sight of blue eyes staring into his.

*What the hell is happening to me?* was his last coherent thought before he drifted off into sleep. That man is going to be *so* much trouble…

## Chapter 8

Leslie stood at the bar, drumming his fingers on the top. It was more of a habit than the fact he was impatient. As he waited for the rather hunky bartender to put his drinks order together, Leslie watched his friends with a fond smile. It was one of those rare nights when all of them could get together and they were gathered at a favourite cocktail bar on the outskirts of Chelsea.

He watched as Eddie mischievously teased his boyfriend Gideon's dark blond, wavy hair into a faux Mohawk. Leslie was sure that no one had ever done that before, firstly because Gideon's hair was longer than it used to be and secondly, because Gideon would probably have bitten their fingers off. Eddie, however, managed to smooth the hair into a short, upstanding facsimile of something similar to Elijah Wood's version and topped it off by placing the umbrella from his cocktail drink in the centre. It certainly looked ridiculous but Gideon was grinning and gazing at Eddie with so much affection Leslie felt a lick of envy. He wished someone would look at him like that.

Next to Gideon sat Taylor, his dark hair waving around his face as he chuckled at Gideon's new look, and his hand reached up idly to tuck his own irreverent curls behind his ear. Taylor's fiancé, Draven, leaned over and smoothed the hair away from Taylor's cheek and then the two men leaned in to each other for a kiss hot enough to melt metal. Leslie's dick twitched at the sight of the two men so obviously enjoying themselves.

"And here I am, the bloody fifth wheel on the bus. It sucks."

There was a chuckle from behind the bar and Leslie turned to see the bartender smiling at him.

"Did you say it sucks or you suck?" The barman enquired with a cheeky wink. "'Cos if it's the latter, I wouldn't mind testing it out."

Leslie returned the grin. He liked being hit on. It gave him confidence that the universe was in balance.

"Oh, I don't know about that," he said airily as he picked up the tray and turned to join his friends. "Maybe I'll catch up with you later." He blew a kiss at the barman and sashayed his way across the floor with his drinks tray. He deposited the tray on the table and sat down beside Eddie.

"I'll get the next round as well," he said with a wink. "The bartender is pretty cute." He picked up his lime daiquiri and took a long slurp.

Eddie chortled. "Go for it, Leslie. He is hot." He eyed the bartender closely. "Really hot. He has arms that could—" He squeaked as Gideon took hold of his ear and twisted it. "Hey, don't be like that. I'm allowed to look, aren't I?" He cast an injured glance at his lover.

Gideon released his ear. "Look, not drool. I'll need to give you a damn bib if you inspect him any closer."

Draven let out a bark of laughter. "He does look as if he works out a lot. Nice chest." He leered at Taylor. "But you're much hotter than him."

Leslie blew a loud raspberry. "Look at you trying to get some." He affected an American accent which he thought wasn't half bad. "Butter me up, baby, 'cause I am *so* gonna to get laid tonight…"

Taylor chuckled. "You mean he doesn't already *every* night?" He rolled his eyes and nodded at Draven. "The man's insatiable. I only have to bend down and he's like, oh Taylor, shall we indulge in a little bit of hanky panky…"

Draven smirked. "That's because you're hot, like I said. Don't go putting all the blame on me either. You're the one who hides handcuffs all over the house 'just in case.'"

Taylor's face turned darker, which meant he was blushing under his caramel skin. "Fuck, Draven, don't tell everyone about that. Honestly. You have no damn filter."

Leslie listened to the banter, the sense of loneliness at times like this intensifying. He was really happy for Eddie and Taylor having found the men of their dreams, but he wished he could do the same. That thought made him think of Oliver and he had a sudden yearning to call him. He put down his drink and stood up quickly.

"I need to make a phone call, guys. I'll be back in a moment."

He ignored his friends' cat calls and dirty comments about phone sex and made his way to the quieter front lobby of the restaurant. He looked at his watch. Ten p.m. Surely it wasn't too late to call Oliver? He squashed down his misgivings and dialled the number which he already knew by heart. They'd been texting each other and even had spoken a few times. He knew there were only two more days to go before their dinner 'date' but he really needed to hear Oliver's voice again. The phone rang a few times and just as Leslie was about to disconnect the call, it was picked up.

"Hello?" Oliver's voice was thick, sounding sleepy and Leslie mentally kicked himself. It sounded like he'd woken him up.

"Hi, it's Leslie." He knew the phone would show an unknown caller as Leslie always suppressed his number after his stalking incident.

"Leslie? Is everything all right?"

"Yes, everything's fine. I just wanted to call and say hello." He shook his head in shame at that lame response. Normally he was pretty eloquent but Oliver made him a little stupid. "I hope I didn't wake you up."

"I was watching a film. I might have dozed off a little so I'm glad you woke me. Are you calling to cancel our dinner thing on Friday?"

Leslie was horrified. "No, not at all. God no. Why, do you want to cancel it?" His stomach had butterflies at that thought.

Oliver gave a low, sexy chuckle. Leslie remembered hearing that exact noise on a Nicky Starr movie he'd watched (they were fast becoming an addiction) in the last week and his cock grew hard.

*Down, you poxy thing. I can't go back to the table with a hard-on. Those guys notice everything.*

"No, Leslie, I don't want to cancel. I'm looking forward to it. A little nervous about going out in public to somewhere that isn't one of my safe places, but I'm willing to take the chance."

A wave of relief swept through Leslie. "Oh, good. Me, too. You'll be awesome. I mean, the date will be awesome, although you will, too, of course." He closed his mouth, wondering why it was that this man turned him into a babbling idiot.

"What are up you tonight then that you called me?"

"I'm just out with some friends at the moment, having a drink or two. I feel a bit out of things actually because everyone has their significant other with them." He sighed. "Although the bartender has hit on me, so I suppose that's a good sign I still have my mojo."

"The bartender hit on you? You might get lucky tonight then."

Leslie didn't think he imagined the tinge of jealousy in Oliver's voice and he hugged that thought close as he smiled crazily into the phone. "I s'pose. Anyway, that wasn't why I called. I just wanted to say hi."

"I'm glad you did," Oliver said quietly.

There was a comfortable silence then Leslie sighed. "Well, I guess I should be social and get back to the crazy bastards currently trying to build a pyramid on the table with their drinks. I'll see you Friday then?"

"Yes, I'll be there. I won't let you down."

"Friday it is then. Night, Oliver."

"Night, Leslie. Thanks for the call." The phone went dead and Leslie knew he had a stupid grin on his face a mile wide. He sashayed back to the table.

Taylor looked at him knowingly. "You called Oliver, didn't you?"

Leslie's jaw dropped open. "Get out of here, how did you know that, did you see something in that head of yours?" He narrowed his eyes. "And you do know he's a secret, right?" He huffed. "You were supposed to keep it to yourselves, guys. Not tell the boyfriends."

Gideon snorted. "Good luck with telling Eddie something and expecting him to keep it a secret. He let it slip that you'd met Nicky Starr and all I had to do was tickle it out of him. As well as another thing I did to get him to talk." He smirked. Eddie flushed and went a deep pink.

The whole table erupted into laughter.

"No, you daft bugger, I didn't 'see' anything." Taylor grinned. "It's just that whenever you say his name, you get this goofy look on your face. You had the same look when you went to make your phone call. And don't worry; none of us would ever spill the beans about him. You know that."

"You've got it bad for this guy, Leslie," murmured Eddie with a smile. "Are you falling for him?"

Leslie tossed his head haughtily. "We're just friends."

There were more hoots around the table. "Yeah, we believe that one," Taylor scoffed. "Like we believe you didn't send that blow-up dinosaur to Gideon for his birthday."

Leslie fluttered his eyelashes and affected a southern accent. "Well, I do declah, sir, you have me all wrong. I swear on my pinkie finger that I did not send that big, green, six-foot dinosaur to this man, and I will swear that 'til my dying day."

Gideon snorted. "You bloody little liar. You might have gotten someone else to post it but I know it was you who sent me that damned monstrosity." He shivered in remembrance. "All green and fuck, it glowed, too."

Eddie snorted drink out of his nose and for a moment everyone was distracted as they cleaned up the beer that had sprayed over the table. Leslie grinned. Laverne had had the time of her life posting the horrible thing to Gideon. The post office worker had blushed as they'd stood there filling in the recorded mail slip that said what was contained in the box. They'd been fairly vocal about their 'package,' which had led to more lewd jokes. Leslie was still surprised they hadn't been kicked out of the premises.

He looked around at the people closest to him, his heart warmed by the sight. He was very lucky to have such good friends and was really looking forward to introducing them to Oliver one by one. He intended to try and bring the man back into the world again and hoped that in the process, something would happen between them that wasn't just friendship.

A man could hope couldn't he?

## Chapter 9

Oliver leaned back in his chair and burped loudly.

Leslie burst into a fit of giggles. "Oh God, excuse my pig; he's a friend," he said to the man sitting at the next table. The man smiled benevolently and continued eating what looked like grilled salmon.

Oliver grinned, his face alight with mischief. "Sorry about that. The food is just so damn good, I was showing my appreciation."

Leslie smiled back at him. At first, Oliver had been nervous upon arrival at the restaurant, hanging behind Leslie as he walked into Galileo's. After meeting Gideon, who had been at his most charming and who'd personally escorted them to their intimate table in the corner behind a wooden screen filled with fragrant red flowers, Oliver had finally begun to relax.

He was dressed in a pair of black chinos, coupled with a white, open-necked, long-sleeved shirt which hugged his muscled frame like a wetsuit, with a black-and-white-striped waistcoat, closed, but for the top two buttons. Leslie was definitely a fan of the look. Oliver's wavy blond hair was artfully styled and held in place with gel, and the scar Leslie knew was there was hidden behind thick strands that framed his handsome face.

"I told you he was a great chef. Your prime rib looked really tasty. I have to say my calamari was delicious." He sipped his third glass of wine. He was feeling rather mellow. The man across the table looked incredibly sexy and Leslie was really beginning to get impatient. Yes, he knew the whole 'let's be friends' thing was a start, but honestly? His dick was raring to go and get Oliver into bed. He didn't think his libido would hold out much longer. It had been on high alert ever since seeing Oliver standing outside the restaurant, looking slightly overwhelmed. The sheer vulnerability of the man had struck a chord in Leslie's tender heart.

He didn't think he was mistaking the looks that Oliver was throwing his way either. They were hot, wanton glances of need that Leslie felt were probably reflected in his own eyes. He knew Nicky Starr's preferences in men, having read his interviews and watched the movies, and Leslie definitely fell into the 'right type' category. That was his ace in the hole, he decided while he observed Oliver over the rim of his wine glass, chatting animatedly about a new website design he was doing for some mega new porn star.

Leslie was exactly what Oliver Brown was looking for. The man just didn't know it yet. Or rather, he knew it but wasn't ready to act. It was going to be up to Leslie to get things moving along and he decided the time had come to try his luck.

His foot gently brushed against Oliver's under the table, and he was gratified when he started, seeing his dinner partner's eyes heat up as he took a sip from his whisky glass. Leslie took it one step further and ran his booted foot (he hadn't worn heels tonight, preferring to ease Oliver into that side of him a little more gradually) teasingly along Oliver's calf.

His lips curved in a smile that said Leslie was courting trouble. The sight of those rich, pink lips around the rim of the glass, and the amusement in his eyes that said Oliver knew full well what was going on, made Leslie as hard as adamantine. He saw the Nicky Starr persona behind Oliver's casual lick of his lips; his narrowed eyes were almost alive with hunger.

"Bit of a twitchy foot, there Leslie?" Oliver said softly, his tone dangerously seductive. "You might need some medication for that condition."

"Oh, sorry, did I touch you? My bad. I was just getting…a little uncomfortable. I needed to stretch."

Oliver nodded slowly. Leslie felt the slow stroke of a shoe against his left leg, a gentle sweep that made him want to rip off his clothes and beg Oliver to take him right there. Manfully, he controlled that impulse. Gideon would be as pissed as hell if he didn't.

The two men stared at each other over the remains of their dinner, each silently acknowledging that things were changing between them.

"So," Oliver drawled as his foot crept slowly up Leslie's thigh. "Do you think perhaps we should get the bill and get out of here? Back to my place, perhaps?"

Leslie swallowed, finding it hard to speak as that wandering foot nudged his groin. Said groin was on fire.

"What about the friends thing?" he squeaked, all the while wanting push his crotch into the foot causing him such turmoil.

Oliver's mouth curved in a wide, sexy grin. "I kind of think that's a little passé now, Leslie. I am so damn horny if I don't have you soon, I'm going to come right here at this table. You have no idea how bloody sexy you look," he murmured huskily.

Leslie knew he'd dressed to kill in his tight black jeans with a huge dragon buckle, a tight wine-red tee shirt, teamed with a black suit jacket with fine red stripes. But the lust and desire in Oliver's eyes made him quail a little. This was a man who had lapped at other men's arses for a living and then fucked the daylights out of them. As much as Leslie had his fantasies, he was a little overwhelmed at that thought.

"You look spooked." Oliver sat back, the moment gone, his eyes wary. "I'm sorry. Did I come on too strong?"

Leslie leaned forward in panic. "Oh God, no, everything's fine. Sorry, I just had a brain fart moment, thinking about us, together. It sort of overloaded my circuits."

Oliver laughed softly, the tension in his body easing. "I thought you were having second thoughts."

"Oh, hell no. I want to go home with you. I haven't been able to think of anything else. I'll ask the waiter for the bill then we can get a taxi back to your place?"

That course of action duly agreed, soon Leslie and Oliver were in a taxi heading back toward his house. Despite the intimacy of the under-the-table shenanigans, Oliver was subdued as they sat in the back of the taxi. Leslie really wanted to get close to him, press his own lips against those only inches from his, but something warned him to not to push it. Oliver was in full defensive mode, folding his arms across his broad chest and gazing out of the window.

It was only when they were inside Oliver's home and the door had closed behind them that Leslie got his wish to see and feel the man the way he wanted. He had only taken two steps inside when he found himself being yanked into Oliver's strong arms, and a hot, wet, greedy mouth found his in a frenzy of want. There were no lights on in the hallway other than a soft glow emanating from a room nearby.

"God, you drive me crazy," Oliver growled as he propelled Leslie toward the open door and shoved him through. Leslie nodded eagerly, his mouth too busy kissing any part of Oliver he could find.

Somehow he ended up on his back on the large, soft couch with the strong, firm body of Oliver on top of him, rutting against him.

Frantic hands scrambled at his jeans and Oliver cursed as he realised the barrier between them.

"Button-down jeans? No easy peel zipper?"

Leslie stared at him aggrievedly despite the fact he was as eager to get out of his pants as Oliver was to remove them. "I love my 501s. Much more fashionable. They, oh fuck." His serenade of the benefits of the button fly was interrupted as Oliver managed to get some of the buttons undone and reached inside and took him in hand. His mouth lunged at Leslie's who could do nothing but lie there in the soft lamplight and be ravaged.

Strong fingers tangled in his hair as he kissed the crap out of Oliver, and Leslie floated in a sense of bliss. The scent of the man on top of him, his hardness digging into Leslie's groin, the feel of lustful lips on his and the roughness of stubble on Leslie's skin were all conspiring to send him out of his mind. He reached down and unzipped Oliver, desperate to feel that hardness in his hands. Oliver gave a heartfelt groan as Leslie's fingers gripped his dick tightly, and his mouth grew even more ravenous. When they finally came up for air, Leslie's lips were swollen and his brain completely scrambled by his lover's greedy tongue and the rough strokes on his dick. He'd never felt so taken and assaulted and wanted in his life, and he loved it.

"You haven't had any for a while, huh?" Leslie managed to get out between hungry, sloppy kisses and Oliver's hand roaming all over his body, yanking up shirts, and rubbing his passion-hot skin.

"Christ, it *has* been too damn long," Oliver panted as they stroked and mauled each other. "I'm sorry I'm not going to last enough to fuck you right now, Leslie, but we have all night. I want so badly to be inside you, but I need to take the edge off first."

And that thought sent a thrill through Leslie's groin and his dick exploded with creamy spurts of come that flooded his designer jeans and his groin, and he gave a strangled cry, pressed his mouth hard against Oliver's neck, and bit down in the throes of his orgasm.

*Yup, I'm a biter. Hope you can deal with it, Oliver.*

Oliver yelped as Leslie's teeth nipped skin and then he threw back his head and roared. Warm fluid coated Leslie's hand, the scent of sex in the air overpowering. Oliver collapsed against him, both of them sticky and replete. Leslie closed his eyes to savour the fact he'd just jerked off Nicky Starr, his personal wet dream. Satisfaction radiated through his limbs and he smiled against Oliver's sweaty shoulder.

"Wow," Oliver murmured. "Sorry that didn't quite go as I had planned, but I…you know, needed that. Needed you."

"Needed you, too," Leslie sighed. "That was pretty awesome anyway. I can't wait to see what else you have to offer." He shifted uncomfortably. "Not that I don't like you on top of me, but you're pretty heavy. Do you think…?"

Oliver pushed himself upward with one powerful move of his left arm and hovered above Leslie. He leaned in and gave him a gentle kiss. "Your wish is my command." He rolled off and lay beside Leslie, on his back. Leslie unthinkingly reached out a hand to caress his face and move damp strands away from his eyes.

Oliver pulled back with a grunt. "Don't do that please."

Leslie dropped his hand and gave a deep sigh. "Oliver, I don't care about the scar."

"I do." Oliver's tone was uncompromising. "It's the only thing off limits. Don't touch my face."

Leslie's heart ached at the vulnerability behind those words. "So you can stick your tongue in the back of my throat, but I can't touch you there? Oliver, you are one incredibly sexy package and the scar is part of it. Part of who you are."

Oliver's eyes darkened in the dim light. "You don't know me well enough yet to know who I am, Leslie. You might not like the man when you truly get to see him in all his damaged glory."

Leslie sat up and looked at Oliver, his brows lifting. "Really? We've just had hot, mad monkey sex of a sort and you start getting all maudlin on me? I think I must have lost my touch. Normally guys tend to be a little more upbeat after sex with me." He hoped his attempt at levity might lighten Oliver's mood. His lover snorted and Leslie thought it was with amusement and not anger at his forthrightness.

"I think that's probably very true." Oliver's fingers lazily trailed down Leslie's semen-sticky stomach. "You're the sexiest man I've ever seen. And my good intentions at just being friends went out the window when you started playing footsie with me under the table."

It was Leslie's turn to snort now. "Oh, I think we both know that whole friends things wasn't going to last too long."

There was a comfortable silence then Oliver raised himself on one elbow and brushed warm lips over his forehead. "Maybe we should clean up then get into bed. It's a damn sight more comfortable than this couch."

Leslie pursed his lips. "I don't know. I'll have fond memories of this couch. Being manhandled by a sexy porn star has always been a fantasy of mine."

Oliver stiffened and Leslie wondered what he'd said. Oliver's next words cleared it up.

"So you're only here with me because I was a porn star?" He sat up and catapulted off the couch angrily. "It's Nicky Starr you want then?" he spat as he stood above a wide-eyed Leslie who wondered what the hell had gone so suddenly, horribly wrong. "Well, I'm sorry, but I'm all out of porn star. The only thing that's left is a damaged Oliver Brown." He zipped his chinos up with trembling fingers.

Leslie knew this was a make or break moment and he swung his legs around and stood up.

*God, this man is so broken.*

Oliver watched him with both fire and uncertainty in his eyes. Leslie reached him and enveloped him in his arms, tightening his grip when Oliver tried to pull away.

"I didn't say that," Leslie whispered into Oliver's ear. "I said Nicky was the fantasy. You're the real deal and I know who I'd rather have. Oliver Brown. The man in my arms, the one whose heart I can feel beating—that's the man I want. Stop being so damn prickly. I know I say the wrong thing sometimes—I wouldn't be me if I didn't—but you're going to have to learn to live with it if you want to be with me." He nibbled on Oliver's ear. "I'm a package deal. You get the kooky with the sexy."

He took a chance and leaned away, then framed Oliver's face with his hands, hoping he wouldn't be pushed away. "You're pretty special just as you are. And I think you should take me to bed now and fuck the daylights out of me. I have a hankering to meet Mr. Brown up close and personal."

Oliver sighed deeply and rested his forehead against Leslie's. Leslie did a mental fist pump that he'd gotten to touch Oliver's face without incident. That had to be good sign.

"I'm sorry," Oliver muttered. "I'm not used to this sort of stuff anymore. I…"

Leslie didn't let him finish, just stuck his tongue in Oliver's mouth and proceeded to mine it. His lover responded with a moan, gripping Leslie's hips and grinding against him.

*Good God, the man is already hard. How the hell does he do that? I guess in his past profession he got it trained like a performing monkey.*

The thought made Leslie giggle and Oliver pulled away in confusion. Leslie didn't have the heart to tell him that he'd just compared Oliver's prick to a monkey, so instead he went back to mining. His own cock was starting to come to life again, and the thought of a bed and perhaps even getting to stay over for the night and wake up to him was a real turn-on.

"We need to get to bed," Leslie panted as he pulled away from Oliver's seeking mouth. "I need skin, flesh and your cock in my arse. What do you say?"

Oliver seemed not to need encouragement. He took Leslie's hand and dragged him up the winding stairs to the top landing. Leslie was unceremoniously pushed into a bedroom, a lavishly decorated royal blue and burgundy concoction of satins, cottons and plush armchairs; thick, heavy curtains and a chandelier in the middle of ceiling that took his breath away.

He stared at it in awe. "Oh my God, you are *such* a porn star." Immediately, he clapped his hands to his lips and turned to Oliver. "Oh crap, I'm sorry, my mouth ran away again."

Oliver put his hand across Leslie's mouth, his eyes dark with hunger. "Strip," he commanded. "I want you naked on my bed, right now."

Leslie was faint with the thought of being shagged and hastily he disrobed, feeling a slight prickle of discomfort at leaving his already crusty clothes in a heap on the floor. When he turned around, now stark naked, Oliver's smile turned wolfish as he took in Leslie's hard-on and naked body.

"I think I said get on the bed," he murmured gently, eye-fucking Leslie from top to bottom. "I'll get the stuff we need."

Leslie nodded and climbed onto the bed, lying face down, rubbing his cock shamelessly against the silk of the duvet. He didn't care that he was staining Oliver's cover. All he knew was that the fabric felt good against his swollen and heated skin and he moaned a little as he writhed in pleasure. There was a choked gasp behind him and he looked back over his shoulder to see Oliver watching him, lube and condoms in hand, his face twisted in lust. His hair was mussed, but still it covered the scar. Leslie had a plan for that later, to get Oliver to be less self-conscious about it. He also saw for the first time the twisted skin that ran down the outside of Oliver's right arm, and the thin scars that bisected the same side of his torso. None of that mattered to him.

"Fuck, you look so hot," Oliver said as he leapt onto the bed and straddled Leslie's calves. "You have the perfect arse, you know that? Tight and just waiting for me."

Leslie shivered, those words causing goose bumps to form on his over sensitive skin. "It could be the heel-wearing," he mused. "I like to exercise my butt muscles when I wear them and dance. They say it's a good way to tone up." A hot body covered his and he closed his eyes in bliss.

"You wear heels?" Oliver's tongue licked at his ear. "That is fucking sexy. I love that image." His voice was husky, full of desire. "Will you wear them for me one day? Let me fuck you in them?"

Leslie's heart filled with joy. He had a picture of himself on his phone in a corset, hat and heels. He'd have to show it to Oliver one day and get his engine even more revved up.

"Oh, God yes," he exclaimed as Oliver's tongue trailed down his shoulder blades and back. He gripped the bed sheets tighter at the sensation. "I have this pair of red ones you'll like, and…oh, hell yes…" His voice tailed off in pure pleasure as Oliver parted his arse cheeks and lapped at his hole. Then the bliss of having fingers inside him, opening him wide, rendered him speechless. He gyrated and made little mewling kitten noises as Oliver proceeded to probe his hole, pushing his tongue inside him with wet, sloppy sounds that made Leslie's cock throb.

He lost himself in the feeling of being explored, dominated and well and truly prepped. When he felt the cool dribble of lube at his hole and between his cheeks he sighed in relief and pushed his backside toward the man currently taking him to such pleasurable heights. When his hips were pulled up and Oliver's cock nudged his entrance, Leslie pushed back and groaned as it sank deep inside him.

"Are you okay, Leslie?" Oliver's husky voice was strained. "Tell me if I hurt you."

Leslie huffed loudly. "Just bloody get going, will you? I'm chafing my cock rubbing against this silky stuff, but it feels so damn good. And you inside me...God, it's heaven..."

There was a warm chuckle behind him and Leslie arched his back as Oliver began pounding into him in earnest. The smooth slide and slap of flesh was a welcome sound in the room, as the two men moved together, finding each other's rhythm. The unsteady movements caused them to grunt and swear in equal measure.

Leslie was lost in the moment and when Oliver reached around, his breath hot against Leslie's ear, and took his cock in his strong hand and jerked him with smooth, practiced ease, Leslie gave a cry of delight and came all over Oliver's satin cover. His body trembled, his skin prickling with heat and his balls contracting as he spewed forth what seemed like a never-ending stream.

Behind him, Oliver continued pounding Leslie's tender hole then tensed and gave a strangled gasp as he bucked against Leslie's arse, clutching his hips with fingers that Leslie was sure would make him bruise. His lover collapsed against Leslie's back, sinking him down into the wet, sticky pool beneath his stomach.

The strong, erratic beat of a heart against the skin of his back made Leslie smile as he closed his eyes and let the lethargy of their lovemaking take over. Oliver was heavy and he couldn't really breathe, but he felt so good plastered across Leslie like a second skin. It was only when he realised that actually, he *couldn't* breathe, that he began to panic a bit and gasp.

"Do you mind getting off me so I don't expire in the wet spot?"

Oliver grumbled as he unpeeled himself. "I was comfortable there. Why do you have to make me move?" he whined as he thudded down next to Leslie, staring up at the ceiling.

Leslie turned onto his side to stare at the man beside him. "I don't fancy being carted out of here covered in come even with a big smile on my face," he teased. In the intimacy of the moment, he took a deep breath and reached out to Oliver's face. Oliver watched him, eyes vigilant. "Plus I wanted to do this, please let me," he whispered as he moved the hair back from Oliver's face and shifted up so he could kiss the scar that showed. Surprisingly, gratifyingly, his lover flinched but didn't recoil or push him away. Leslie trailed his lips down the damaged flesh, a gentle kiss that ended at Oliver's mouth.

"There," he said softly. "See, you're not the monster you make yourself out to be. You're stunning, honestly." He touched his lips to the scar on Oliver's arm, kissing from wrist to shoulder.

Oliver swallowed and stared at Leslie with eyes that shone wet in the dim light. "Gregori said I was."

"He said you were what?" Leslie stopped his tour of Oliver's arm and snuggled into his side.

"Said I was a monster, because of the way I looked after the accident." He shrugged one shoulder. "But he was pretty mad with me at the time."

Leslie wanted to kill Gregori Golovin. "How could he say that to you? And especially when you were hurt?"

"He was an arsehole. A complete and utter bastard. I just didn't realise it until it was too late." Oliver stared up at the ceiling and Leslie reached over and wrapped an arm across his chest. His lover's skin was still sweaty from their lovemaking and his heart beat erratically beneath Leslie's outstretched arm.

"About three weeks before the bike accident, I found Greg dealing E to some kids." Oliver's voice was quiet, but anguished. "And when I mean kids, I mean twelve, thirteen-year-olds."

Leslie's insides churned. "Hell," he whispered. "I suppose as an adult it's a choice you make to take drugs. I don't agree with it but...kids? That's just disgusting."

Oliver nodded in the dim light. "That's what I thought. It's one thing me going off half-cocked and killing myself slowly with coke, but to deal to children? That was a new low, even for Greg." He shifted in bed and Leslie stroked his matted chest and waited for the story to unfold.

"I threatened to tell the film studio about it, get him kicked out. I was a bigger star than he was so they would have done what I asked." He snorted drily. "It was another thing that pissed him off about me. That I was more popular."

"Why the hell did you stay with a man like that?" Leslie reached up and caressed Oliver's cheek. "You deserved better than him." He snuggled closer into Oliver.

There was silence for a minute. "I loved him." Oliver stroked the top of Leslie's head softly as Leslie's heart beat faster at those words. He'd known Oliver had feelings for Gregori, but hearing him actually voice them hurt a little. "He was everything to me at the time and I guess I was willing to look past the cruelty and the bad times. We did have some good times. Just not that many."

He sighed heavily. "Anyway, he told me he wouldn't do it anymore. I believed him. My first mistake. Then Leo found him with an eleven-year-old kid who hung around the studio, selling him baggies of all sorts of stuff. Leo told me. He didn't like Gregori at all and he'd have done anything to get him kicked off the set." Leslie heard the smile in Oliver's voice. "He said the same thing as you. That I was better than Greg and deserved more."

"Leo was a clever man," Leslie murmured as he moved across Oliver and his lips kissed a soft path down his chest.

His lover chuckled. "Like you, you mean? Little brat." He hitched a breath as Leslie moved lower down his body. "You're not helping. How am I supposed to tell you this story if you keep doing that?"

Leslie waved an airy hand. "Oh, you'll cope." He blew a raspberry on Oliver's stomach and grinned at his lover's surprised exclamation. "I'm doing my bit to ground you here, so lie back and enjoy it."

"I'm not so sure about grounding me," Oliver murmured. "I look ready to take off."

Leslie sniggered as he palmed Oliver's rising cock, causing him to gasp. "I'll climb aboard in a little while, Captain. Go on, tell me the rest."

He looked up to see Oliver watching him with an expression that took Leslie's breath away. It was a look of longing, of need so intense Leslie wanted to board the aeroplane right that minute. Instead, he held himself back and sat up, crossing his legs, sitting Buddha-like at the bottom of the bed.

"There. No more distractions. Carry on. Tell me the rest."

Oliver snorted softly. "*You* are one big distraction." He reached over to the side table and took a sip of water. When he put it down, his face was once again serious.

"I had to tell the studio about it. I didn't want to, I knew Greg wouldn't react well and it would fuck up our relationship. But I didn't have a choice. I wasn't about to let him get away with ruining kids' lives. Reggie, the owner, didn't take it well. He'd lost a brother to drugs so he had a bit of a bug up his arse about it. He hated us using drugs but he knew he couldn't stop it. But when I told him about Greg dealing he went ballistic and gave him notice. He was kicked off the set and told not to come back."

Oliver fell quiet.

After a while Leslie spoke. "Is that when you two broke up?"

Oliver nodded. "It was the beginning of the end. I kicked him out of the flat we shared, and he and the twins, he had these two sycophants that used to hang around him, moved in together." His tone was guarded and Leslie wondered what Oliver wasn't telling him. "I didn't want to stay there anymore so I went to stay with Leo for a few weeks until I found another place." He waved a hand around him. "This house. I wanted something outside of the city centre and this fit the bill." He gave a twisted smile. "My principles broke us up, I suppose. And the house certainly came in useful after the accident. No one really knew about it, so I had the privacy I wanted."

Leslie scooted up over him fiercely, straddling his hips as he looked down. "Your humanity broke you up, Oliver. And his selfishness and arseholiness."

Oliver gave a soft snort of amusement. "Is arseholiness even a word?"

Leslie nodded emphatically. "Oh, definitely. It's *my* word." He laid himself flat on top of Oliver and took his mouth in a deep kiss. Beneath him, Oliver's cock moved and Leslie grinned into the kiss. When he sat up, he ran his hands down Oliver's stomach.

"Permission to come aboard, Captain? I have a feeling this is going to be a short flight."

Oliver's husky tone sent a shiver down Leslie's spine. "Permission granted."

## Chapter 10

In his persona as Nicky Starr, Oliver had revelled in the chance to go out on the town, wear the suits he adored and flirt with anything that moved, male or female. Of course, he'd never have taken the offers from women wanting to 'convert him to the dark side' seriously. He was far too into guys for that. However, flirting was a natural tendency with him, no matter what gender. And you never knew where it might get you. It had defused a few difficult and sensitive situations. However, looking across at the darkened face of Katie, sitting opposite him, he didn't think flirting with her would work to reduce the ire she currently sported.

"You are so full of shit," she snapped. "I don't know why the hell you talk such crap about yourself." Katie picked up her wine glass and took a gulp. "That man adores you, anyone can see it. It's just you who are too bloody minded to let him in and accept that someone can actually like you." She slammed the wine glass down on the restaurant table, slopping the contents messily onto the tablecloth. It was a quiet lunchtime at Fidalgo's and the place was not too busy.

Oliver scowled. "It's my opinion. I'm allowed to have one, aren't I?" He started when she snorted and threw her napkin at him. It hit his chest then dropped onto his lap. He picked it up and chucked it onto the table. "Wow, that's mature. Next we'll be having a food fight."

"Don't bloody tempt me. I still have some bourguignon left in my bowl."

They glared at each other and it was Oliver who dropped his eyes first. "I just said he can do better," he muttered softly.

He'd been seeing Leslie for the entire month since their dinner. They'd spent time together having satisfyingly mind-blowing sex, and Oliver had even managed to go to a couple of movies with Leslie, since they sneaked into the darkened theatre when the lights were off and generally sat in the back and made out.

Leslie told him he didn't mind the scar, or the fact Oliver's damaged eye tended to twitch a little when he got tired. He'd cut Oliver's hair to what he called 'a more flattering style' and Oliver agreed that while it still covered the damage, it did look better. He'd tentatively offered to wear concealer over the scar when they went out. Leslie had just kissed him and told him that if Oliver wanted to do that for himself, it was fine, but he didn't have to do it for him.

"I know what you said, you idiot. And you know I don't agree. And neither does he from the way he looks at you." Katie and Leslie had met each other recently when they'd all met for coffee. The two had hit it off straight away.

Katie's tone was a little less hostile now and she reached out and placed one plump, bejewelled hand on his. "Listen. I know better than anyone what that twat Gruesome Gregori did to you. I know how much he hurt you. But he was wrong. You deserve the very best, you know that. And Leslie has been good for you. He's a keeper."

Oliver toyed with his fork and didn't look up. "Exactly. He's cute, sexy, gorgeous, on his way up in the fashion world…did you know he was actually head-hunted from Debussy's by one of the huge Burberry stores but he refused to leave? He's intelligent, funny and lights up a room when he walks in. That's why I say he needs someone without the baggage, someone he can have on his arm that goes to all these fashion shows with him and isn't afraid to be seen in public."

"And he makes you happy," Katie said softly. "I've not seen you like this in two years, Ollie. Not since that bastard of an ex-boyfriend did such a number on you."

The use of the diminutive for his name—something Oliver wasn't partial to, but tolerated from Katie—warned him he was about to get the *talk*. The same one Katie had been giving him since he left the hospital, broken in both body and spirit, by a man he'd thought had once loved him.

"Don't start," he warned Katie. "I'm not in the mood for the whole rah-rah speech today."

"Fine. I won't say how much I hate that bastard for what he did to you in hospital. Or how I'd love to string him up by the balls and wallop his fat arse with a cat-o'-nine-tails. Or tell you that you are definitely a great catch and he missed out on the chance to be with a great guy…" She waggled her eyebrows and Oliver couldn't help chuckling at the expression on her face.

"You just have to have the last word, don't you?"

She nodded, eyes sparkling. "I'm a woman, dahlink. Of course I do." Her face grew more serious. "Have you told Leslie anything about your ex yet?"

Oliver's chest tightened. "He knows about the drug bust thing, and Greg getting chucked off the film site. I haven't told him much more."

No, he hadn't told his current lover about the fight he and Greg had after Oliver told the studio bosses about the drug dealing. Or the fact that his boyfriend had beaten him so badly that night he'd needed a week to recover. Or that the night he'd had the accident, he'd come home to his London apartment to find his ex-boyfriend (he hadn't gotten his key back yet) impaled by Pierce—one of the twins—as the other twin, Payton, fucked Greg's mouth. There had been a ménage of note going on in Oliver's own bed.

He'd escaped their taunts and insults, their laughing derision and drug-fuelled aggression and found a party where he could drink and forget and then…the accident had happened. And Gregori's cruelty hadn't stopped after that either.

"Hey, you okay, honey? You're looking terribly pensive all of a sudden. I'm sorry if I'm going on. I just love you, and I want you to be happy."

Oliver managed to twist his face into a smile. "Yeah, I'm fine. Can we stop with the memories now and think about something else?" He smirked and reached for his phone. "Leslie showed me this new Salad Fingers video, maybe you'd like to see it?"

Katie shrieked in horror. "Oh God, please don't. You know that damn thing scares to me death. It's so creepy. That guy has to be completely psycho to make such twisted stuff."

Leslie had introduced Oliver to the character and he'd become hooked.

He laughed loudly. "It's just a drawing, Katie. I find them kind of funny myself."

"You two are just weirdoes. You deserve each other." She grinned at him and finished her wine, motioning for the waiter to come over for another order.

Oliver chuckled. "I have something else that will make you laugh. Remember we went to Galileo's for dinner on Valentine's Day?"

Katie nodded, a wistful look on her face. "You have to take me there, Oliver. I'm dying to see this place."

Oliver reached over and took her hand. "I'll make a plan, I promise. Maybe for your birthday we can get a group together. Anyway, Leslie has this friend called Eddie, Gideon's boyfriend. He's this amazing chef and honestly, his pistachio ice cream is amazing."

He took a sip of his drink, smiling as he recalled the events of that evening. "He's also got a bit of a reputation for being a klutz. Really nice guy, sexy, too, for a redhead, but a bit like a gangly Dalmatian who's been let loose." Oliver sniggered. "He came over to say hello, talking and waving his arms all over the place and managed to knock some poor guy's toupee off his head." He laughed out loud at the memory of the restaurant patron's red face and Eddie's stammered apologies.

Katie let out a peal of laughter as she snorted wine all over the table and Oliver. "Oh my God, that must have been so damn funny." She wiped her mouth with her napkin.

Oliver grinned as he dabbed white wine off his shirt. "Yep. Gideon was like a master of urbanity, like, 'So sorry, sir, accidents do happen, and please have the meal on the house,' while glaring at Eddie and Eddie looking like a puppy who had peed on the carpet. It was hilarious. And Leslie was too damn adorable, with that snorting thing he does. I love it when he laughs like that."

Katie reached over and squeezed his hand. "You realise when you talk about Leslie, you get this look on your face and your voice changes? Oliver, that's all the proof I need that you two are so absolutely right for each other."

Those words still rang in Oliver's ears when he got home that night. He wasn't so sure Katie's words were true.

*  *  *

The loud cry of distress behind him caused Leslie to drop the bale of cloth he was busy stacking and jump about a foot into the air. He clasped a hand to his chest as he saw his boss's face staring at him in horror.

"*Oh. My. God.* Laverne, what the hell is wrong with you? You made me pee my pants a little."

Laverne strode over to him, appearing to be hyperventilating—badly. "Is that my Dormeuil *ikonic* fabric lying on the floor with the dust and the mouse droppings? Oh please tell me it isn't."

Leslie glanced down at the floor where the bale of exorbitantly expensive grey suit fabric lay. "I can't tell you that," he said guiltily. "Because it is."

Laverne shrieked and Leslie winced. For a man, Laverne could pierce the eardrums.

"Leslie, you need to pick it up right now." Leslie was sure his boss even stamped her foot a little like a diva-esque My Little Pony.

Leslie gently kicked the bale he'd dropped to the side and walked over to the errant cloth. He leaned over and hoisted it up, holding it in his arms then laid it out on a nearby cutting table. As Laverne opened her mouth to say something, Leslie placed a finger to his lips telling her to *shh*. Laverne's eyes narrowed and as she moved toward him rather threateningly, he took up a soft cloth and began dusting the fabric gently. Out of the corner of his eye, he kept a cautious look out for his boss in case he got hit around the head with a handbag or perhaps just Laverne's large hand.

"Sorry, poor baby," he murmured to the material as he caressed it gently. "I'm sorry I left you all alone down there, among all the muck. I mean"—he raised his voice slightly—"I know there are no rats or mice in here, so there's no poo on you, but you deserved better. Let's get you cleaned up and on the shelf where you belong."

Laverne looked slightly mollified as she bore down on Leslie like the Titanic. "This carelessness just isn't like you. You've been a bit distracted lately. Is everything all right?" At the thought of just how all right everything was with Oliver, Leslie grinned to himself. His arse was still sore from last night's activity, and their Valentine's Day celebrations.

"I knew it, you're getting laid," Laverne chortled. She tapped the side of her nose. "A little bird told me you were seeing a certain customer of ours with the initials OB. Is that true?"

Leslie gaped at her. "What? Who told you that? How…" His voice tailed off at Laverne's deep chuckle.

"Oh, sweetheart, Laverne gets to know everything. You mentioned his name once in passing then went all gooey eyed. I had to find people in the know and get the full story." She waggled a finger at him. "I told myself then he was something special to you, not just a delivery." She grinned wickedly. "Although he may be that, too. I was waiting for you to tell me about him yourself, but I saw I'd just have to pry it out of you."

Leslie flushed and tried to keep his air of insouciance. "God, you are one big gossip bitch, girlfriend."

Laverne's eyes softened. "Oliver is someone special, isn't he?"

Leslie didn't kid himself. "Yes, he is," he admitted. "I really like him."

*I even think he could be the one.*

Leslie knew he was falling hard for the blond-haired, moody and insatiable Oliver Brown. They'd spent a lot of time together, but he just wasn't sure whether Oliver felt the same. The man had a way of hiding his thoughts and emotions and sometimes Leslie felt there were two distinct people inside him. The Oliver who was warm, tender and laughed at Leslie's jokes, and loved it when he wore his heels to bed, and the other, darker Oliver, who was morose and sullen and looked at Leslie as if he didn't quite understand what he was doing there. Leslie didn't like that side of his Oliver at all.

He looked at Laverne, a niggling feeling of worry in his stomach. "Is it okay to see Oliver?" he asked haltingly. "Because I don't want it to become a problem at work."

"Oh, honey, it's fine. Do I look like an ogre? As long as you don't sell my suits to him for nothing to sweeten him up to play with that cute arse of yours, it's fine."

"Oh." Leslie heaved a sigh of relief. "Thank you."

"Well, I'll tell you a secret." Laverne leaned in, her pink lips curved in a slow smile. "I've been seeing a guy, too, this really sexy, gorgeous guy, and we've hit it off a few times if you know what I mean."

Leslie's ears pricked up. "Oh, you have? Anyone I know?"

Laverne shook her head. "I doubt it." Her eyes took on a starry look. Beneath the female persona, Leslie knew the man, Lenny James, was something of an incurable romantic. Lenny was one of those people who simply believed the best of everyone and everything.

"We've had dinner a couple of times and then, you know." Laverne grinned.

"So, he's met you as Lenny then? Does he know about Laverne?" Leslie asked the question innocently, but wasn't prepared for the shadow that crossed Laverne's eyes.

"No, he only knows me as Lenny James. I haven't introduced my other self to him yet. It's still early days, you know? I want to ease into it."

Laverne sounded suddenly shy and Leslie reached over and hugged her tightly. "Well, you're both awesome people so he can't help but love you both."

"I hope so," Laverne mused, her face a little worried. "He's quite an old-fashioned guy, a little set in his ways. Brook has this charm about him…" She stopped, suddenly conscious that she'd let slip his name.

Leslie laughed. "Don't worry. Your secret is safe with me. I won't tell anyone about Brook." He broke into song. "Laverne and Brook, sitting in a tree, K-I-S-S-I-N-G." He leapt nimbly out of the way of Laverne's raised hand coming down to thwack him across the head and scuttled over to the other side of the cutting table. Unfortunately he slipped on a wayward swatch of silk on the floor and went barrelling down onto his arse, frantically trying to stay his fall by clutching at the table. Alas, that didn't go too well, as all he got was a handful of suit fabric, which came flooding down like a wave and covered him like a swaddling blanket. He lay on his back on the floor, winded and unable to see much through the dark material. He did hear Laverne's hearty, unmistakeably male, guffaws of laughter.

"Oh God, that was too precious. I wish I'd had my video camera on that. I would have made myself £250 easy with *You've Been Framed*. Leslie, honey, you just made my day. Are you okay under there?"

More wails of laughter rent the air as Leslie tried to extricate himself from the cloth, which was threatening to suffocate him. He finally stood up, trying to retain as much dignity as he could, despite having hair that stood on end and a face that felt as red as a beetroot. It wasn't his most auspicious moment.

"I'm fine, thank you." He swept his hair back from his forehead haughtily. "My hair needs a Valium after that escapade, but the man who is Leslie Tiberius Scott is ready to go. Now if you'll excuse me, I really need to pee."

With that, he swept past a still-chuckling Laverne and escaped to the bathroom to repair both his hair and his decorum.

On his way home that night, he heard a loud whistle and his name being shouted from the construction site next door. He looked up to see Frankie's cheeky face beaming at him from a ledge about twenty feet up.

"Hey, sexy man. How are you today? Loving the outfit, by the way."

Leslie preened at the compliment. He had to say his dark blue pinstriped suit and pale blue shirt did make him look rather natty.

"Hi, Frankie," he called.

The labourer grinned. "When are you going to join me for a drink at the pub?" he called out. "Just as friends. I know you're spoken for."

Leslie smiled up at him. The man had been trying to get him go for a *friendly* drink for weeks. Frankie was a big, affable man, a few years older than Leslie, with muscles and a wide smile, a cute, boy-next-door face and a swathe of dark brown hair that fell over his forehead. It had become a bit of a tradition for them to meet up when Frankie had his smoke on the pavement below as Leslie left work. Leslie smirked. He rather thought Frankie waited for him and then dashed down to see him right on time. Leslie might have Oliver, but the attention of another guy was always welcome. Even if he was a smoker. Leslie didn't like smoking.

"I heard you and some of the guys were invited to the fashion show on the fifteenth March? Laverne said she'd given you some tickets. Maybe we can catch up then?"

Leslie was working hard on getting both the show and the event organised with his boss and he didn't think Oliver would come, as much as he'd like that.

Frankie went on. "Yeah, me and my mate Stewart are coming. Not really our thing but we get to dress up in pretty clothes and have a few free drinks and eat some good food, so we're in. Plus you're there." He flashed a wicked smile down at Leslie. "That makes it even better."

Leslie flushed. "Okay, then, I'll see you there. It should be a really good event." He waved as he continued walking by him. "See you tomorrow."

"See you, gorgeous. It's the one highlight of my day. I wouldn't miss it for anything," Frankie teased.

Leslie grinned at that and sashayed down the pavement with an extra sway in his hips. It was always nice being appreciated.

# Chapter 11

Oliver stared moodily into his soup as he drew the spoon around in circles, sloshing the liquid over the side of the bowl. He'd been having major problems with a website that he was building and he'd needed a break. The tin of tomato soup for a later dinner had seemed like a good idea, coupled with crusty day-old bread, but now he just thought he should curl up in a dark corner and sleep. He knew it was all down to his bad mood and the sheer capriciousness of the current internet connection he had, as he vaguely remembered that he'd seen a notice somewhere that his service provider was working on upgrading the lines in the area. He hadn't paid much attention to it at the time.

He was also suffering from withdrawal symptoms at not having seen Leslie for the past few days. His lover had been busy at work, organising some future fashion show or other, and had been working nights and weekends to get it sorted.

So when the doorbell rang, he didn't scramble to answer it. Perversely, he ignored it. He wasn't expecting anyone and it was probably some door-to-door salesman. He did peer out into the garden, but it was dark and he could see nothing. The doorbell rang again, more insistently as if someone had their finger pressed on it. Oliver growled loudly.

"Fuck off, will you? Can't you tell I'm not here?"

His mobile rang. He scrambled to pick it up and his heart leapt when he saw it was Leslie. *This* summons, he answered.

"Leslie, hi. I thought you were working tonight."

Leslie sounded rather exasperated when he replied. "I managed to get the rest of the night off. Instead, I thought, you know what, I'll go and pay a surprise visit to my boyfriend. So I doll myself up and rush post haste to his house only to find he's not answering his bloody doorbell!"

Oliver shot up from his chair and dashed to his front door, phone melded to his ear. He was surprised in a number of ways. First, that Leslie was here. Secondly that he'd called him his 'boyfriend.' They hadn't got to that discussion in their six-week relationship yet, and he was both a little scared and exhilarated at the term being used.

"I'm on my way," he blabbered. "Sorry, I thought it was a salesman or something. Hold on."

He reached the door, turned the lock then yanked the door open. His jaw dropped, the phone left his shoulder and clattered to the floor.

"Holy shit," was all he could manage. His cock managed much more than that, going from droopy to sledgehammer in about two seconds flat.

Leslie smirked from beneath eyes rimmed with guy-liner, his full lips pink and pouty with clear lip gloss. He wore a black coat, open in the front, under which he slayed, killed and worked a dark grey corset, which clung to his slender figure as if painted on. Teamed with sheer black stockings and red stiletto heels, Oliver had never seen a more erotic sight in all his life. And, given his former line of work, he'd seen quite a few.

"Can I come in then?" Leslie's husky voice made Oliver's dick jump and he nodded speechlessly.

"You came across town looking like that?" Oliver gaped. "Leslie, that's a bit dangerous, isn't it?"

Not to mention he didn't want anyone seeing his lover dressed like *that*. This was for his eyes only.

"Oh keep your pants on," Leslie drawled as he sashayed into the house. Then a wicked grin flashed across his beautiful face. "Or not…and don't worry. I didn't wear these shoes across town." He waved his man bag at Oliver. "I had jeans on and a pair of flats. I changed just before getting here."

"Changed where?" Oliver said dazedly.

"There's a coffee shop about four houses down. I popped in there and did the deed. So, are you happy to see me?" He licked his lips lasciviously as he cast a glance at Oliver's crotch. "I'd say that's a big, fat yes."

Oliver closed the door and tried to control the urge to rip Leslie's clothes off and drag him caveman-like into the bedroom. "Of course I'm happy to see you. I missed you these last few days."

Leslie's face softened and he drew Oliver into a fragranced hug. "I missed you, too, sweetie." His lips found Oliver's in a tender kiss, gentle and loving and Oliver succumbed to the sublime creature in his arms and sighed happily into his mouth. When they drew apart, Leslie grinned at him.

"That's more like it." An expression of uncertainty flitted across his face. "Oh and hey, I just realised I called you my boyfriend back there. It just sort of slipped out. I quite understand if you don't want me to call you that…"

Oliver reached out a finger and held Leslie's lips closed. "It's fine. That's what we are, isn't it?"

Leslie's—his *boyfriend's*—eyes shone and the smile on his face would have lit the whole of London on a dark and dreary night. "I'd hoped so."

They looked at each other and Oliver realised that at that moment, something had changed. He was terrified by the realisation that someone had come to mean more to him than he'd ever wanted—which meant he could be broken again. He quashed the squirming fear inside and waved toward the lounge.

"Shall we have a drink, you can tell me about your day and then perhaps I can peel those stockings off your legs. And that corset… fuck, you look incredible."

Leslie waved airily, a pink flush suffusing his cheeks. "A drink sounds like a good idea. For now." He smirked and walked past Oliver with a waft of fresh-smelling eau-de-cologne.

When they were settled with drinks and light chill-out music playing in the background, Leslie settled back into Oliver's arms with a happy sigh, his legs stretched out sexily in front of him.

"This is the life," he declared. "I had such a rough day at work, but you make it all okay."

Oliver loved hearing about Leslie's days at the fashion house. There was always something going on, some quirky tale to tell. He was having a tough time not pouncing on his boyfriend, though.

"Tell me all about it. Did any more material try to attack you?" he murmured, as he drank in the scent of Leslie's shampoo and watched his elegant legs fidget around getting comfortable. He'd enjoyed his lover's last dramatic account of the fabric that had 'tried to eat him.'

Leslie huffed. "No, that was a one-off, thank God. But Laverne has been on this mission with this latest fashion show to really make her mark. As part of the show, she had me practicing draping fabric over all these naked statues on the catwalk. That way she can see what look she wants on 'the night.'" He warmed to his subject. "I mean, I seem to have become her *go-to* toy boy. I thought I was the fabric buyer, not the set designer and general factotum." He scowled adorably and Oliver hid a grin. He knew Leslie *loved* being included in anything to do with the fashion house, but sometimes he felt he simply had to make a fuss.

"What kind of statues?" he asked idly as he ran his fingers through Leslie's hair.

His boyfriend's eyes lit up. "Naked ones, like David, you know? All these mock guys in all their glory. I have to drape the material strategically over them. Later, part of the show will be when the models release the fabric and reveal what's underneath. Some sort of Grecian fantasy Laverne is putting together. It looks really cool. I wish you could see it."

Oliver's heart skipped a beat. His earlier bad mood had disappeared seeing Leslie at the door in that sexy getup. Perhaps he could take their excursions a step further. Give himself a little bit of shock therapy and see how he fared.

"Do you mean that?" he said quietly. "If I decided to come down and watch the show, would that be something you'd want?"

Leslie swung around and stared at him. "I'd want? Oliver, you know I'd love to see you get out to a function like this, show everyone you're around." He gave a slow smile. "That you're mine."

Oliver's dick liked the idea of being Leslie's. His heart did, too. "No promises," he warned. "But I do think I owe it to you to try and be a little bit more public. Get over this whole recluse thing." His insides quailed at what he was proposing. "Just get out and about a bit, let people see I'm around. I mean, it's not like they think I'm dead or anything, and people still see me when they go the shops and shit, but at a fashion show a lot of people I knew once will recognise me."

"You don't owe me anything," Leslie said quietly. "I understand you're scared at what you think people will say. But honestly, you really don't look that much different. It's only in your head that you see the change, think it's worse than it is. That's what I've been trying to tell you." His hand reached out and caressed Oliver's cheek. "If you want to come with me, it would be awesome. I'd love it."

Leslie grew more animated. "I could get Laverne to put a little table at the back for you, and you could sit there like the mysterious stranger and let people wonder who you are. Maybe even wear a masquerade mask over your eyes, like the ones in V for Vendetta.

Ooh, I could even get Draven to be your official bodyguard. He can stand there beside you with that glower he has making sure people can't bother you. Taylor would love that, seeing his man all dangerous and tough. I bet it would mean Draven would get a lot of nookie when he got home."

Oliver was laughing at the flow of words from Leslie's beautiful mouth so he shut him up the best way he knew how. He kissed him. Kissed him with all the feeling he had for this whimsical and quirky man-child, this man who made his heart beat faster and his soul soar. He knew it hadn't been that long, but he knew he was falling fast for the irrepressible Leslie Scott.

Leslie sighed and kissed Oliver back with fervour, soft lips nibbling at his, hands reaching in and touching skin. The soft whisper of Leslie's stockinged legs against Oliver's own made Oliver crazy with want.

"Please," he whispered. "Undress for me so I can see all of you. Naked is your best outfit, Leslie."

Leslie smiled wickedly and stood up. He wandered over to the DVD player and fiddled about with it. The soft, sensual music of Beyoncé's 'Dance for You' began to play. Then he bent down, arse to Oliver and removed one of his high-heeled shoes, slowly, tantalisingly, in time to the music. The corset tugged up and his tight, round cheeks made Oliver's mouth water. He watched the sexy, lithe and limber form of his lover perform a strip show of note as Beyoncé wafted through the speakers. Leslie's eyes closed as he removed his shoes, waving them teasingly at Oliver as he lay feet up on the couch. So turned on, Oliver was afraid to move in case the simple friction of his cock against his underwear and pants made him come. He wanted to savour the gorgeous man gyrating languidly in front of him, appreciate every moment and then make love to him, taking his time, breathing in Leslie's moans, which would become music to his ears.

Leslie mouthed the words to the song as he danced, then reached behind him and began undoing the clips to his corset. Oliver was so hard he was like the proverbial diamond in an ice storm. Slowly, teasingly, the vision in front of him taunted and teased, eyes half closed, as Leslie removed the garment. The corset was carelessly whipped to one side and Oliver lost his breath. His lover wore a tiny black thong underneath, the fabric already stretched and wet with arousal by Leslie's own hard-on.

"Liking what you see?" Leslie asked huskily, his eyes never leaving Oliver's. "See how I dress for you? Only for you, I promise." His face promised Oliver delights and Oliver so wanted to take advantage of them. He reached down and pushed his jeans and underwear off, throwing them to one end of the couch. Hastily, he pulled his shirt above his head until he was naked. He held the base of his cock tightly as Leslie undulated in front of him, rolling his stockings sexily down his legs. Oliver didn't want this to be over too soon. But, the lustful look in his lover's eyes as his hips and shaved crotch moved closer toward the couch was clear. Oliver's mouth wanted to take Leslie's beautifully upright cock in and show him just what he thought of his strip tease.

Slowly, Leslie stepped out of his not-really-there thong, and stood swaying to the finishing bars of the music as Beyoncé's voice tailed away. The sight of the man naked was one Oliver would take to his grave. Coltish, long limbs, an elegant yet strong build, a face that could sink ships with its open-eyed beauty and legs that looked as if they should be wrapped around Oliver right now.

"Put those heels back on and come over here," he growled. "I need you. So damn much."

The soft smile Leslie gave him was like the sun coming out on a grey day. Teasingly, he slipped his shoes back on, tantalisingly waving his beautiful ankles at Oliver as he did so. Then he moved over to Oliver and straddled his hips, his cock only inches from Oliver's yearning mouth. Slowly, Leslie eased forward until the tip touched Oliver's lips and he took him in, revelling in the musky taste, the smooth and heated flesh who was his lover. Leslie gasped and pushed deeper into Oliver's mouth. He loved it when Leslie fucked his mouth, loved the sounds he made, needy and desperate as those blue eyes watched his own cock moving in and out as Oliver's tongue and lips paid homage to the beauty that was Leslie Tiberius Scott.

The music continued to play in the background and Oliver closed his eyes and surrendered to the feelings building in his chest. This was something sublime, something to be savoured.

He got into his teasing torture, and not too soon after, Leslie's hands gripped his shoulders tightly, hips rocking as his panting grew louder. Oliver smiled around the cock in his mouth. He knew Leslie's breaking point, the point at which he could no longer hold back. He decided it was time to end it, as his own cock wanted inside Leslie so badly he didn't think he could last much longer. His tongue dipped into the slit, and his mouth tightened, and sucked and Leslie gave a cry of bliss and came hard. Wet, sweet-tasting come flooded Oliver's mouth and dribbled down the side. He relished every drop as Leslie slumped forward, holding Oliver's head tightly against his sweating belly.

"Oh God, every time you do that, I swear it's the best ever," he groaned as Oliver kissed the skin over his mouth. "You are just so good at it."

Oliver shrugged as he moved his head away so he could breathe and not be smothered by toned abs. "Plenty of practice," he said cheekily and Leslie laughed as he shifted position.

"Oh yes, Mr. Porn Star, that's definitely one of your best talents."

"I have other talents," Oliver murmured. He frowned. "You taste sweet. How come?"

Leslie chuckled. "I read this article that says incorporating fruit into your diet makes a difference. I tried eating pineapple and berries this week. Obviously, it worked." He waggled his eyebrows as he positioned himself above Oliver and stared down in amusement. "Maybe we should try different flavours, see if it's true? I could eat curry all week, then seafood and maybe you'll be able to taste the difference."

Oliver grimaced. "I'll skip the seafood and curry thanks. I rather like fruity Leslie."

Leslie laughed loudly. "Oh, I'm fruity all right. Don't you know that yet?"

"Fruity and the sexiest man I know," Oliver said huskily. "Now do you think we can get back to what we were doing? This hard-on isn't going away by itself."

"Your wish is my command," Leslie whispered as he picked up the tube of lube on the nearby table. There was always lube somewhere in Oliver's house. He figured it was an occupational hazard.

One of the things Leslie liked to do, and Oliver loved to watch, was to use his fingers inside himself as he readied himself for

Oliver's cock. He made these strange grunts and sighs, and his face scrunched in pleasure.

"One of these days, I'm going to do this to you," Leslie murmured as he squirmed above Oliver. "I know you're not much of a bottom, but I really want to be in your arse at least once or twice."

Oliver nodded, his eyes feasting on the sight in front of him. "I've bottomed before. You know that, just not recently. But there is nothing I'd like better than you inside me. I'm ready when you are…"

Leslie used Oliver's sweats to wipe his sticky hands, tossing the pants on the floor once he'd finished. Grabbing a condom, Leslie unwrapped it with a quick, wicked grin and slid it onto Oliver's ready dick, sheathing him, making sure to flick his leaking tip as he did. Oliver heaved a shuddering, needy sigh at the contact. When Leslie finally straddled Oliver, teasingly lowering his body onto his cock, they both gasped, and Oliver gave a groan of satisfaction. He held back the impulse to push upward, and instead watched as he disappeared inside Leslie's eager hole. Wet heat engulfed his sensitive flesh as Leslie's fingers rested on his chest. Leslie rode Oliver gracefully, in balletic movements that were fluid and focused, his sexy heels adding to the sheer eroticism of his movements.

"My God, you do that so well, " Oliver gasped as his hips began thrusting impatiently upward as he strived to bury himself as deep inside Leslie as he could. "You are wicked, you know that?"

Leslie's reply was to bounce even harder on Oliver's dick, twisting his nipples and gripping skin until Oliver succumbed to the sight and sensation as he and Leslie became one. It seemed to Oliver that all those moments spent as Nicky Starr, all those sessions with men he'd knew as friends, colleagues or didn't know at all, were nothing compared to the moments of completeness he felt when he was with Leslie, making love.

The feeling of belonging was amplified as his groin exploded, his skin prickled and the orgasm that thundered through his body rocked his world. He clutched at Leslie's slim hips and bellowed out his satisfaction.

Leslie leaned back, resting his hands on Oliver's thighs and moaned. "I have two words. Fucking. Awesome. I love to make you flip like that. God, you look so damn sexy when you do."

Oliver's heaving chest needed air so he took in some deep breaths. "You are going to bloody kill me."

Leslie's soft laugh made his dick twitch—just a little. "Not the intention. Dead body sex is so gross. I need you alive and horny." He lifted himself up, expertly removed the condom, tied it…then flung it on the side table. He slipped off his shoes and laid them gently on the floor.

Leslie winced as he settled next to Oliver on the couch, feet tucked up beneath him. "Why do we always seem to end up on the couch when we do this? I don't think we've made it to the bedroom more than about three times since we met." He nestled into Oliver's side, gently tracing the scars on his body with warm fingers.

Oliver chuckled tiredly as he wrapped an arm around his lover. "Because you do things to me that no one has ever done before. Drive me to distraction."

Leslie moved up onto one elbow and stared down at him, brow furrowed. "Really?" He sounded uncertain. "I'd have imagined you'd have had another man in your life that might have made you feel that way. Gregori Golovin didn't do that?" He bit his lip. "Sorry. Bad form talking about an ex-lover to your present one especially after mind-blowing sex."

Oliver's stomach had lurched at the mention of his ex. "Greg never made me feel like you do." He stopped, not really wanting to tell this story now, but feeling it was due. "Greg was controlling, very charismatic. I was only twenty-one when we met. I was flattered that a man like him would be interested in someone like me. He was dominant, strong and I enjoyed that aspect. I was crazy about him."

Leslie's soft breath brushed his ear but he said nothing. His hands simply stroked Oliver's belly and torso, grounding him.

"We had some good times. But when I got him chucked out the studio for the whole drug thing, he turned really nasty. He'd always had a violent streak in him." He took a deep breath. "He beat the shit out of me that night. I needed a week to get over it. He'd hit me a few times before then, and apologised. I always took him back. Like an idiot."

"That bastard," Leslie growled. Even in this emotional state Oliver thought it was as sexy as hell. "Honey, you thought you loved him. That plays havoc with your common sense. I can't believe he beat you that badly, the prick. I'm never watching his films again." The determination and disgust in Leslie's voice made Oliver laugh.

"He may look like a blond god with those green eyes and platinum hair but he could be very cruel. I found out just how much the night I went back to my apartment, after we broke up and found him there with two other guys, the twins, remember I mentioned them before?" Leslie nodded against his shoulder. "I'd forgotten to get my key back." He fell silent as he remembered. "Greg was there being spit-roasted by these two guys. He didn't even care that I was there, seeing it. They just carried on. I screamed and ranted and they laughed at me."

Leslie's hand tightened on his shoulder. "Fucking bastards," he murmured. "I hope you stuffed them up."

Oliver's chest tightened. "I should have done, I suppose. I didn't." His voice was hollow in the quiet of the room. "Instead I rushed out, found my own party, got doped and boozed up and went on a motorbike ride."

Leslie sat up swiftly. "That was the night you had the accident? Oh, Oliver."

The grief in his voice made Oliver pull his boyfriend down closer into his arms as he kissed his fragranced hair. "I was a fucking idiot. I shouldn't have done it. I can only blame myself."

"Maybe, but you weren't thinking straight. God, I wish I could kick that motherfucker in the balls with my heels." Leslie growled again.

Oliver smiled at the feral sound. "I love it when you do that," he chuckled. "It's pretty hot."

Leslie smiled against his skin. "I'll have to do it more often then." He kissed Oliver's chest softly. "What happened after the accident? Did Gregori at least come to see you in hospital, say he was sorry?"

Oliver laughed harshly. "Oh, he came to visit me all right. I was in and out of consciousness, all doped up on all kinds of shit. I woke up to find him there, sitting by the bed." He paused, remembering the gladdening of his heart that perhaps everything was okay again, that Greg had come to ask forgiveness and wanted him back. "I told him I still loved him, needed him. He just smiled and leaned down and said that now I looked like a monster, there was no way anyone would ever want or need me again."

Leslie's horrified gasp echoed in his ear.

Oliver's chest ached with pain. "He told me that I was a pathetic, useless fuck-up and that I was finished in the porn industry because the only way they'd be able to pay anyone to fuck me was with a paper bag over my face." He smiled twistedly. "Then he left."

The room was silent. Against his chest, Oliver heard a muffled sound and he reached down in surprise to lift Leslie's face to his. His lover's eyes were wet with tears and he was vainly trying to hold back a sniffle. "Leslie, honey, please don't cry. It's all over now, and I have you, remember?" Tenderly he smoothed locks of Leslie's damp hair off his wet cheeks.

*I have you for now, at least.*

"I can't believe someone would say something like to you when you're all busted up in hospital," Leslie sniffed. "He's such a tosser. I am definitely burning all my films with him in. Then I'm going to pack them in a box and send him a letter telling him what I think of him. It will include the words *fuck you* and *twat*."

Oliver laughed. "You do that, you devil, you." He was warmed at the reaction to his story, that Leslie cared about him that much. Warmed and scared at the same time. He was back at his old *I'm getting too close to this man* scenario, the one that meant he could end up getting hurt again and hurting Leslie in the process. That was his biggest fear.

*I'm not the right guy for a bright, shining star like Leslie to have a future with. What if I can't be what he wants, what he needs? Maybe my own damn insecurities are going to drag him down, and he doesn't deserve that. He's too special to have anything but the best in his life.*

They lay together, quiet, each busy with their own thoughts. And when Leslie reached up again with wet, salty lips and claimed his in a fierce, possessive kiss, Oliver closed his eyes and let all the bad memories of the past fade away for a fleeting, wonderful moment.

## Chapter 12

Oliver loved lazy Sunday mornings. Especially when he woke up with Leslie curled beside him. There was something about having his lover's pert, warm arse snuggled against Oliver's already aroused body that really made it worthwhile sleeping in. He smiled and kissed the back of Leslie's neck, making him chuckle softly and wriggle against his already hardening dick.

"Someone's ready to go again," Leslie murmured sleepily as Oliver ran a hand though his messy bed hair. "Wasn't last night enough for you? You made me come so hard I saw stars."

Oliver trailed his lips across the bare skin of Leslie's shoulder. "I could never get enough of you," he murmured as his lips trailed down the soft skin of his boyfriend's back. "You're this irresistible force of nature who I have to contend with."

Oliver loved the way the body in his bed arched back, and Leslie's languid arm reached back and pulled Oliver's mouth to his for a hot, slightly stale-breath-smelling kiss. Morning breath really didn't matter when it was Leslie's.

For a moment they lost themselves in the shift of skin on skin, the press of a cock between firm, willing cheeks and the promise of something in passionate kisses and questing tongues. The moment was lost when the doorbell rang.

Oliver lifted his lips from Leslie's and frowned. "Who the hell can that be? It's eleven a.m., for God's sake." They waited with indrawn breath and the doorbell rang again.

"Well, whoever it is, they aren't going away," Leslie murmured as he settled back down on his pillow, with no intention that Oliver could see of getting up to answer the door. Since it was his house after all, he wasn't surprised when Leslie said, "I s'pose you'd better go see who it is." He snuggled back under the covers and closed his eyes.

Oliver muttered as he got out of bed and pulled on his sweatpants. "Bloody rude of them coming at this time of the morning."

There was a snort from under the covers and Oliver leaned over and swatted Leslie's arse hard. The squeal that followed made him smile. He wandered out of the bedroom, down the hallway to the front door. He yawned and scratched his belly.

*This had better be something damned important.*

He definitely wasn't expecting what he found on his doorstep. Packaged in a slender five-foot-seven frame with styled dark hair, twinkling dark brown eyes, a cheeky grin and bearing a McDonald's bag, Maxwell Lewis was not someone Oliver thought to see.

"Hi Ollie, long time no see. I come bearing gifts. Can I come in? I only just got in from the flight from Mexico and oh my God, worst ever. I had some woman trying to grope my balls all the way back. And let me tell you, spending thirteen or so hours in the air with some crazy chick feeling you up, that is *so* not cool. Can I come in? Did I ask that already?"

The complete diarrhoea that flowed from his friend and sometimes-bed-partner's mouth, coupled with the hated diminutive of his name had Oliver reeling. Maxwell beamed at him and pushed him out of the way to come inside and make his way to the kitchen.

"You're looking good, Ollie. Love the whole sweaty bare top, sweatpants thing you've got going on there. Very Brad Pitt. Très sexy. So who is he?"

Maxwell planted the McDonald's bag on the kitchen top, and turned to give Oliver a sly wink. "Can I meet him? Or is that taboo—one fuck-buddy meeting another one?"

Oliver finally found his voice and the welcome gap in Maxwell's verbiage to actually talk. "Max, wow. I didn't know you were in town." He glanced anxiously down the hallway wondering if Leslie could hear. "I have to say I wasn't expecting you."

"Oh, you know me." Maxwell waved a hand airily. "I like to keep people on their toes, surprise them." His eyes narrowed. "And you, my friend, have the freshly screwed look, plus there's dried come all over your chest. Is he here? Can I say hi to him?" He made a move toward the hallway and Oliver knew that Maxwell would have no hesitation in marching into Oliver's bedroom and introducing himself. He barred Maxwell's way.

"Hold on a minute, Max. Dial down the Duracell bunny a notch. You're making my head spin."

Max grinned at him. Truth be told, Oliver was really pleased to see him. He'd missed his quirky friend and part-time lover. Maxwell was one of those people who took every day in his stride, faced it head-on like a relentless juggernaut and didn't do commitments. Apparently, he kept a spreadsheet detailing the name of each of his conquests, with their height, age, weight, telephone number, orientation (top, bottom or side), fuck ranking from 1-5 (5 being the best) and dick size. That way, he'd told Oliver smugly, he could use his pivot table to narrow down whether he'd a) seen the guy before and b) wanted to see him again. The latter occasion was rare. Maxwell had never told Oliver what his ranking was, but he kept coming back for more so he supposed he must be a 4 or 5.

"I'm on an unexpected layover. I picked up some guy in a bar in Mexico City. It turned out he was the married-to-a-woman son of some bigwig who like, almost owns the airline I fly for, if you can believe that, and he's 'in the *closet*.'" He sighed. "The powers-that-be have put me on a four-day leave while they assure the guy I won't be putting the pictures I have of him fucking me onto the net, or the video on YouTube. I am hoping I still have my job though. It'd be a bummer to lose it because of some dickwad who can't admit he likes men." Maxwell gave Oliver a ferocious grin. "I told them if they get rid of me, those pictures and the video will definitely be getting airtime. So I think they saw my reasoning." He stroked his neatly trimmed goatee with a wicked glint in his eyes, looking for all the world to Oliver like an old-time villain in a black-and-white film.

Oliver blinked. It was too early for the likes of Maxwell. The man was a dynamo in bed and out. "Huh. Great story. Well, yeah, I do have someone here, so now isn't the best time for a catch-up. Maybe we can meet at Fidalgo's later...?"

"Oliver, is everything okay?" Leslie's voice echoed behind him and Oliver turned. Leslie stood there, eyes sleepy, sheet wrapped around his waist. His hair was tousled, and Oliver's heart leapt at the sight. He looked so damn beautiful standing there.

"Hi," Maxwell bounded like a puppy over to Leslie and held out a hand. "I'm Maxwell, occasional lover of this guy and others, and full-time slut." He grasped one of Leslie's hands and his boyfriend made a panicked grab at the sheet that threatened to drop. "I just popped in to say hi, and wow, you are really gorgeous. Are those eyes real or are they contacts?"

Maxwell leaned in to peer into Leslie's eyes in admiration. "I think they're real. Oliver, what do you think?" He turned back to

Oliver with an expression of hope on his face. "Is he, like, into threesomes? 'Cause I would so like to…"

Leslie's eyes widened in sheer confusion and Oliver jumped in to rescue him, cutting Maxwell's words off with a hand on his mouth.

"Maxwell, A, they are real, B, no, you can't have us both, and C, you really need to tone it down a bit. You're scaring my boyfriend."

Now it was time for Maxwell's eyes to bug out. "Boyfriend? *He's a stayer*? Oh my God, Ollie, that's awesome. You found someone. I love it. It's about time." He reached over and hugged Leslie tightly, who clutched his sheet for dear life. Then Maxwell reached out and did the same to Oliver, who tried to give Leslie a reassuring look. His lover's lips twitched in amusement.

Leslie seemed to have found his composure after being mauled and inspected like a slab of meat. "So you're Maxwell, huh?" He shuffled forward taking care not to catch his feet in the sheet trailing behind him. "I'm Leslie. So nice to meet you. Oliver's told me…some stories about you. I have to say, it's great to meet the legend."

Maxwell flushed in pleasure. "Legend? Oh how kind." He blew on his fingernails. "If somewhat true." He glanced slyly at Oliver. "I suppose this means that you and me are no longer doing the *hide the sausage* thing? Unless, as I said, maybe we could all…"

Oliver moved forward to stand next to Leslie. "No. Just no, Max. Leslie isn't into that sort of thing and we're exclusive." He placed a possessive arm around Leslie's shoulders. "Leslie is mine. And I'm his. So no sausages are getting hidden other than ours." He grinned at Leslie who grinned back.

Oliver saw Maxwell's face shadow, his eyes darkening. It was only a fleeting expression, but he looked almost sad, a little whimsical. Oliver wasn't used to seeing anything close to that expression on Maxwell before.

"Well, that's put me in my place. I understand. You make a stunning couple, by the way. Ollie, I love what you've done with your hair. Suits you. Glad to see you getting over that whole scar thing. You always looked just gorgeous to me. And I heard you're even getting out and about a bit more? I guess that's due to this lovely man next to you? Well done, is all I can say." He made a moue at Leslie. "I could never get him to go out with me."

"That's because you wanted to drag me to every gay club in town," Oliver remarked dryly. "And every party and social event in the London calendar, all in one night. I don't think I could have borne the excitement." He kissed the top of Leslie's head. "And I'm actually attending my first event in a few days' time. A fashion show. I'm a bit nervous but with this one by my side, I'll be fine."

He kissed Leslie's forehead. Leslie smiled softly and presented his face for a proper kiss.

When Oliver finished his boyfriendly duty and looked back at a rather quiet Maxwell, he was surprised to see a look of longing on his face. It was quickly replaced by the mischievous grin he knew well, but he knew he hadn't imagined the other expression.

Was Maxwell growing up? Did he want a little bit of stability in his life instead of just a string of lovers? Someone to come home to instead of simply bang the daylights out of? Oliver wasn't sure, but he resolved to speak to him about it.

"So…" He gestured to the bag on the counter. "Are those for us then? I hope you bought enough of them because I am damn hungry. And you know I love their breakfast muffins."

Maxwell nodded. "I bought six of each. Bacon and sausage." He rattled about in the bag and laid the muffins out on the counter. "Put the kettle on, Ollie. I need black coffee. I'll have mine then get out of your hair. I'm sure you've got better things to do rather than entertain me." He smirked at them.

"Ollie?" Leslie murmured with a quizzical glance at his boyfriend. "I thought you didn't like that name?"

Oliver scowled. "I don't. But he"—he waved his muffin at Maxwell who was happily chasing a random bit of sausage falling out of his breakfast bun—"insists on it. It drives me crazy."

Maxwell pulled a tongue at him then went back to devouring his muffin. Oliver shook his head as he headed over to make coffee.

*Two of my favourite men in one room. This is a turn-up for the books. I never thought I'd see the day. My now ex-lover with my current one.*

He watched as Leslie and Maxwell chatted, enjoying the sight of the two together.

*I could get used to this domesticity. It scares the crap out of me, but I want it so badly.*

Oliver just hoped his insecurities and demons stayed away long enough to make that happen.

# Chapter 13

The night before the fashion show, Leslie was taking a well-earned night off. He had a myriad of things to do—wash his hair, manscape and make sure his outfit was ready for tomorrow night. He was feeding his fish when his mobile rang. Hoping it was Oliver, he rushed to answer and he grinned when he confirmed it was indeed his boyfriend. Sprinkling a few more flakes of Golden Delicious Fish Food on the top of his tank, and hoping that his fish wouldn't explode from eating too much, he answered.

"Hiya, sexy. It's late, nearly midnight. What are you doing up?"

"Now *there's* a leading question," Oliver purred, his voice sending shivers down Leslie's spine and inflating his cock. His voice was husky and slightly slurred. "I was enjoying some wine, and thinking of you. Thinking of you led to a hard-on and I decided I really needed a hand with it." The sound of rustling clothing filtered down the phone.

Leslie's dick liked that idea. He chuckled and put the now-sealed fish food container back on the table. "Is this like, a phone sex call, or something?"

"Or something," Oliver said silkily and Leslie swallowed at the incredibly seductive tone. He made his way over to the bed. If he was having sex now, he wanted to be comfortable.

"What are you wearing?" Oliver growled.

Leslie looked down at his dark blue Andrew Christians and comfy white tee-shirt. "My blue high-heeled pumps and a thong."

He was damned if he was going to tell Oliver the truth and be *bleh*.

His boyfriend's indrawn breath and moan of desire went straight to Leslie's groin.

"You're wearing that around the house? Jesus. You are one sexy fucker." Now Leslie heard the sound of flesh against flesh and he swallowed, his cock inflating.

"Have you got Skype?" Oliver murmured.

Leslie's groin flamed as if he'd suddenly rubbed Deep Heat into his nether regions. "Yes," he squeaked. "I use it to speak to my folks. Oliver, are you beating off?"

His lover laughed softly and Leslie could see how this man had become a world-famous porn star. It was the Nicky Starr sound Leslie had heard so often in his films, a sound so dirty, so tantalising, so damned lust-inducing that Leslie thought he might self-combust.

"Oh honey, you do *not* want your folks in on this show," Oliver murmured. "The things I want you to do for me…"

Leslie looked around for a paper bag, sure he was hyperventilating from the feeling of breathlessness in his chest. His dick was already wetting the front of his underwear, pushing out like the Queen Mary about to set sail. "You want Skype sex? Oh fuck, Oliver. That is so hot. I haven't done that before."

"Good. Your first time can be with me. I can say I popped your c2c cherry."

"c2c?" Leslie fiddled with his laptop as he clicked on the Skype programme to open it. The familiar opening sound made him realise he was definitely doing this. He was going to have sex on camera. The penny dropped. "Oh. You mean camera to camera. I'm just getting it open now. Skype I mean. Hold on a minute."

"Send me an invite. StarrSex69. Hurry up. I'm all set up and ready to go…" There was a low groan and a sudden intake of breath from the other side of the phone.

"Yes, give me a minute. The connection isn't very good. I'll be with you in a sec. I'm going to put the phone off now. Buh-bye. Speak in a sec." Leslie terminated the call and sent the invite and within seconds, it was accepted. He put the call on hold and got to work. He'd never stripped and re-dressed as quick before in his life. He rooted through his underwear drawer for his blue silk thong, slipped it on and then slid his feet into his heels.

He gave a quick look at himself in the mirror, satisfied himself he had nothing stuck in his teeth and he looked good enough for Skype. Then he got back onto the bed and pulled his laptop onto his lap. He hastily clicked the video icon to reveal himself then finally focused on Oliver's profile. When he saw his boyfriend, he definitely needed that paper bag.

Oliver sat in the armchair in his bedroom. His tanned legs were stretched out in front of him, sprawled open and he was naked. One large hand was wrapped around his jutting, pink cock and he grinned sloppily as he saw Leslie. "Hi, sexy. What took you so long? I was thinking about you."

"I love what you've done with that thing." Leslie motioned toward Oliver's cock as he peered closer at the screen. "You're a little drunk, aren't you?"

Oliver nodded vigorously. "Yep, and horny as fuck."

"I can see that." Leslie laughed as he scooted back up to rest against his satin pillows then arranged the laptop strategically just beyond his heeled feet so he could be seen at his best advantage. Luckily it was a nineteen-inch laptop screen—HD to boot—and the picture was excellent.

In the small frame at the corner of the screen he saw himself laid out languidly, his dick bulging in the skimpy thong. Unconsciously, he let his legs fall apart, revealing his arse cheeks. His face flamed with the wantonness of it. He was a slut putting himself on offer and he loved it. He especially loved Oliver's lick of the lips and the hungry expression in his eyes.

"Hell, you look beautiful. That arse…" The longing in his lover's voice made Leslie's skin prickle. Goose bumps formed on his skin.

"Thank you. I aim to please." He palmed his dick and closed his eyes at the feel of the fabric on his swollen, heated skin. "So, you want me to jack off for you to see?"

He squinted his eyes at the screen, thankful his eyesight was 20/20. He saw Oliver stroking himself. The sight spurred him on to wriggle on the bed and touch himself a little faster.

Oliver's throaty growl had him harder in seconds. "Yes. First I want to see you take that thong down, slowly. Then I want to see you get off. I want to see that gorgeous hole, too. Spread your legs more. Imagine me with my tongue in there, licking you, getting you wet, ready for my cock." The commands were softly spoken but there was no doubt who was in charge. Nicky Starr was in the house.

Leslie's whole body was aflame and, as he lifted his legs, he heard a stuttered moan from the other side of the screen. He peeled the thong from his backside, making sure he opened his legs wide, stretching his cheeks apart for his voyeur then lay back again. He was wet, but not enough. He reached over and took out the lube from under the pillow, squeezing some into his hand. Then he slid his fingers up and down his cock, uttering little sighs of pleasure, his eyelashes fluttering as he succumbed to the sensation.

"This feels so good, wish you were here with me. Want to feel your mouth, taste your cock, feel you inside me, filling me…" He opened his eyes and blew a kiss at his lover.

At the foot of the bed, Oliver's breathing quickened, his eyes never leaving Leslie's hand. "God, you look so damned gorgeous doing that. That pucker of yours….I want to be buried so deep inside that you taste me. Want to fuck you so hard you feel me forever. Make you mine and leave my mark."

The dirty words and the soft slapping of Oliver's hand on his cock drove Leslie crazy. He had no doubt Oliver was hearing the same thing on his side. He couldn't stop the grunts and moans that rose and fell from his mouth as he pleasured himself. For a while, he was lost in the feeling of his aching and heated groin and the knowledge Oliver was there with him.

When he opened his eyes, the expression of bliss on his boyfriend's face sent Leslie into a tailspin. He loved to see those half-closed eyes; that look of concentration as Oliver worked himself, and the white teeth that bit into lips he wished he could kiss. The faint sheen of sweat on Oliver's body triggered memories in Leslie's mind of his man, that strong, unique scent that remained embedded in his brain. He breathed in deeply, trying to *will* the smell stronger.

"God, Oliver, I'm ready. Try and come with me."

His arse clenched and his heels dug into the covers as he gasped loudly, and the prickling that started in his toes and ended in his groin and ultimately his dick, intensified. He shouted Oliver's name as he climaxed, his spunk streaming forth, covering his hand, his thighs and his belly. His trembling legs spasmed as his body did the same and from haze-filled eyes, he saw Oliver fisting his cock and spraying his semen in jets that seemed to never end. Oliver's panting and loud expletives made Leslie smile. In true porn style, Oliver was always vocal when he came. Leslie couldn't help chuckling when he saw a blob of spooge sliding slowly down the screen.

"You have some reach, there, cowboy," he gasped out, in between laughing. "Like a damn jet stream."

Oliver's lazy and satisfied smile made his heart beat faster. "Imagine if we ever did it without condoms," he murmured. "You really would taste me. It'd be better than a protein shake." His half-hard cock lay against his thigh as he leaned back in the chair and closed his eyes.

Leslie looked around for something close to hand to clean himself up. Seeing nothing, he huffed and went to the kitchen to pick up a roll of Kleenex and take it back to the bed. Oliver looked as if he were sleeping, slumped in the armchair with a beatific smile on his face.

Leslie watched him, feeling a warmth inside that he knew was far more than simply sex. "Don't you go to sleep on me," he warned. "You know we always talk after sex."

He began to wipe the sticky fluid off his belly and legs.

Oliver opened his eyes and his beautiful amber stare filled with affection nearly made Leslie blurt out the words he really wanted to say. He refrained, not wanting to scare his boyfriend away.

"Not just sex. Making love. Even when we Skype and say dirty, sexy things to each other, we're making love," Oliver rasped.

Leslie bit his tongue. Now wasn't the time for a declaration of love. Not right after *making* love. He didn't think it had the same impact. "I like making love with you. Now you look tired and I have to be up early for the show prep," he said softly. "Go and get some sleep, Oliver. I'll see you tomorrow night."

Oliver nodded sleepily. "Okay. I really enjoyed this little session. We should do it again soon."

"'Kay. Good night. Be sure and wear that suit I picked out for you tomorrow. You look damned fabulous in it."

"I will. Night, love." The screen went black.

Leslie put his laptop back in its customary place on top of his dressing table and got into bed. He snuggled into his pillow with thoughts of Oliver, his warm body and the opportunity to show him to the world tomorrow night.

* * *

Leslie hummed as he straightened the fabric around a rather well-endowed Greek statue and couldn't resist the urge to run his fingers up the stone cock.

"You like that, hmmm?" he murmured as he did it again. "You're as hard as rock; you must do." He sniggered. "I have no idea where Laverne got all of you, but I want one for home. Then when Oliver's not around, I can play with you instead."

"Oh you are one dirty, dirty, boy." Laverne's laugh echoed through the hall. "I might have known you'd be here fondling the men."

Leslie turned and bowed low. "I live to serve. Even statues need a little Leslie-love."

He turned and looked around at the display hall. "It's looking amazeballs, boss. This event is going to be a smash hit."

Laverne scratched her cheek. Leslie grinned at the move. She only did that when she was nervous. "Thanks to you and everyone who got it ready."

The hall did indeed look superb. The models' catwalk made up the centre of the room, and around it were scattered tables and chairs, ready for people to sit down for dinner. One section of the room was cordoned off for press, and the Grecian theme had been lavishly applied wherever possible. Grapes and vines hung from the roof; the statues stood, richly decorated with colourful fabrics from the store room. Huge, mock white pillars stood firm against the walls, and elsewhere, Grecian art and sculptures framed the room on trestles covered with white chiffon. It looked elegant and very posh, indeed.

The best thing about the space, though, was the small two-person table set back from the rest, almost in the eaves of the room. That was for Oliver when he arrived in about an hour. The lights would have been dimmed and although his boyfriend was psyched up to come—he'd talked about nothing else this week—Leslie wanted him to feel comfortable. He knew this was a huge step forward, appearing in public where probably he would be recognised.

"He's going to be fine, Leslie," Laverne murmured when she saw his glance towards the table. "Oliver is really trying so hard to be here for you. He's a brave soul. He must care about you very much."

Leslie couldn't stop the smile that formed. He and Oliver hadn't ever said anything concrete about how they felt, but he knew there was something there, something deep and, he hoped, lasting. "I think he likes me a bit," he said carelessly. "But then, you know, I'm a likeable character, me. Who wouldn't like this sexy package?"

He gestured down toward his Debussy suit, a slim-fitting, pastel blue worn with a matching waistcoat, a blue-and-white-striped formal shirt and a deep blue tie with white polka dots. He even had his favourite tie pin on, a small silver panther Oliver had given him.

Apparently it had been his and he thought it suited Leslie as he was *lithe, mean and sexy.* Leslie wasn't sure how a panther could be sexy, but he loved it anyway.

"You look very handsome, but then it's one of my suits, so I'd expect that," Laverne acknowledged as her eyes dated around, checking the room. "Have you seen Dasher or Bruce? I thought they might be here. I couldn't find them in the dressing room."

Leslie's heart sank. "They are here, though, aren't they? You're not going to make me go down there again and help, because, you know, the trauma last time was enough for me to claim workman's compensation." He knew he was laying it on a bit thick but he had no desire to be at the beck and call of ladies who wanted unmentionable things done again.

Laverne guffawed. "No, Leslie, I won't send you there tonight. Yes, they're both around somewhere. I need to go find them. Camilla was pitching a hissy fit earlier about some fitting not being quite right." She moved away, her mind already occupied with other things from the look of her expression. "Later, Leslie."

Leslie gave a sigh of relief that he wasn't being summoned to the bowels of hell and glanced at his watch. Oliver should be arriving any time, as well as all of his friends. They'd all bought tickets tonight in support of the fashion show to support the Franklin Moore Trust for Homeless LGBTQ Youth, a charity Laverne patronized. He took one last look around the room and nodded in satisfaction. Everything looked superb and he was ready to rock and roll.

"Bring it on," he muttered. "Let's show my boyfriend how we do things in the fashion industry."

\* \* \*

Oliver sat in his chair at the back of the room and watched the crowd around him swell and surge as people greeted each other. It was loud and busy, and he was totally out of his comfort zone. He took another large drink of his red wine and glanced around anxiously. Leslie had promised him he'd be back in fifteen minutes and now it was more like forty-five. The show had been a huge success, the runway models perfection personified and Oliver had to say, he could see a few more suits being purchased based on what he'd seen tonight. He grinned at the thought of what Katie would say about that. She'd been supposed to be here tonight, too, but she'd gotten stuck in Bristol when her plane was delayed and been spitting mad that she wouldn't be there to support him.

He had to admit that putting a suit to go on the town for the first time in a long while had given him a newfound confidence. Leslie had picked it out, fussing through his 'dressing room' (which was simply his spare room kitted with wall–to-wall closing cupboards) and exclaiming in delight every time he found a Debussy. He'd also been delighted when Oliver had pushed him into one of the large cupboards, pulled the door closed and given him a blow job right there.

The deep dove grey suit with the blue-and-white-striped shirt and electric blue silk tie was one of Oliver's favourites and wearing it with a paisley scarf in the top pocket tonight, it looked very dashing, indeed. Leslie had certainly liked it from the smouldering look in his eyes when he'd seen Oliver all dressed up and given him a murmured promise to peel it off him later.

Leslie's friends were über cool. They were all out in force tonight and seemed to be taking turns to check upon him. Gideon and Eddie had wandered over earlier and chatted, and he'd waved at Taylor and Draven as they walked past. It looked like all Leslie's housemates were dutifully love-birded up with only the one stray member of the flock to find his mate. Oliver wished he could say he was Leslie's forever, but his old insecurities were kicking in. Public gatherings like this one certainly triggered his vulnerabilities. However, so far everyone had practically ignored him, apart from a careless glance or quick hello, and he was grateful for that. Perhaps his career as an ex- model and porn star wasn't quite as widely known as it used to be.

He smiled as Taylor sauntered over to him. The man was definitely gorgeous, and Oliver felt a twinge of jealousy that he and Leslie were such good friends.

"Hey, Oliver, how goes it?" Taylor pulled out a chair with a grin and sat down. "I thought I'd come see how you were doing, see where that friend of mine is. He owes me a drink."

"He was supposed to be back a while ago. He's been delayed. Probably Laverne got hold of him."

Taylor chuckled. "Leslie can be a will o' the wisp. He's a real social darling. Everyone wants a piece of him."

Oliver scowled.

Taylor flapped a hand as he laughed. "Come on, you know the guy. He loves to talk." He grew more serious and leaned forward. "I've never seen him this way about anyone before, though. You and he are really getting along, huh?" Dark brown eyes gazed quizzically at Oliver.

"I guess. He's definitely unique."

"Oh that he is. Leslie is one of those who fall for someone, heart and soul." Taylor's eyes met his. "I hope you realise what a special guy he is. I'm pretty protective over him. I wouldn't want him getting hurt."

Oliver nodded. His hand went to his hair in an automatic gesture as he checked it covered his scar for about the tenth time that night.

*Have I just been warned?*

"Yes," he muttered quietly. "He is. Special I mean."

A shadow loomed over Taylor and a large hand clasped his shoulder. Draven Samuels stood behind his fiancé, a wide grin on his face.

"I heard that, Tay. Are you playing best friend 'don't hurt my buddy or I'll hurt you?' Way to make Oliver feel better." He sat down next to Taylor and covered his hand with his.

Taylor smirked. "Was it working? Was I badass enough without overdoing it?" He winked at Oliver who couldn't help smiling at the adoring look the two men gave each other.

Draven cocked his head to one side. "I have to say there's a much better badass side to you, one that we can try out when we get home. I prefer that bad boy." His hand reached out and caressed Taylor's cheek.

Taylor leaned into his hand. "I look forward to that later then." His eyes sparkled as he looked back at Oliver who was feeling both a little uncomfortable and turned on at the wanton expression of want in both their eyes. "I think we're making Oliver a bit nervous. Maybe…"

A slim hand reached out and twisted Taylor's ear. He yowled as he looked up at a glaring Leslie. A surge of relief flooded Oliver's chest as he observed his lover.

"Tay, are you teasing Oliver? I have two words for you. Dressing. Room." His blue eyes flashed a warning and Taylor blanched. Draven looked curious.

"Oh yeah, so not teasing." Taylor stammered, casting a quick look at Draven. "Just getting to know the guy. Look, we'll leave you two lovebirds alone. Draven and I have a dance he promised me. See you later." He pulled Draven away, who looked confused and was mouthing the words, "Dressing room?"

Oliver broke out into laughter as Leslie sat down beside him, looking smug.

"I can't believe you threatened your best friend with that one. I mean any guy in a dressing room is going to flirt with the models, right? Especially when they look like Reuben Tanner." Leslie had told Oliver about Taylor's recent flirtations when Leslie had dressing room duty from hell.

"He had it coming." Leslie smirked. "I knew I could play that card sometime. And it worked."

Oliver leaned forward and kissed Leslie gently. "You're awesome. And, have I told you yet how bloody beautiful you are tonight? The most incredible man here." His kiss grew deeper and he pressed his tongue against Leslie's mouth, loving the sound his lover made when he kissed back. For a moment, the din, hustle and bustle of the room went away and there were only soft lips, hot mouths and seeking tongues. When they pulled apart, Oliver was gratified to see Leslie looked a little dazed.

"God, you kissed me, right here in front of everyone."

Oliver shrugged, feeling like he'd just run a mile and won a medal. "I did. I wanted to show everyone you belong to me. That I'm yours."

"Oh." Leslie's happy whisper went straight to Oliver's groin, which was already hot and bothered. "That's…so…" Oliver hadn't seen a Leslie lost for words before. Apparently a PDA did that to him.

"Anyway, where did you get to? I missed you."

Leslie's brow furrowed and his eyes darkened. "I met someone I know and we got talking, and then time slipped away from me." He reached over and lightly ran his fingers down Oliver's shirted arm. "And now I need to go and make sure all the prizes are ready to be awarded for the raffle. Laverne's a bit nervous about going up on the catwalk to announce the winners; she doesn't really like going in public like that. So I said I'd check they were all ready, so she doesn't make a fool of herself up there."

"Oh. Okay. But hurry back." Oliver reached over and framed Leslie's face with his hands. "When this evening is all over I'm taking you home and I am going to make love to you until you forget your name. I'm so glad you invited me here tonight. I've enjoyed it."

He kissed him again and then looked into Leslie's wide blue eyes. The emotions he saw there both scared and elated him.

"You'd better get off before your boss comes looking for you."

Leslie nodded and stood up. His face shone with mischief. "Now I have a boner, you dickhead. You'd better make sure this gets put to good use when we get home. Maybe this time I'll be the one on top."

With a grin and a wave, he disappeared into the throng. Oliver watched him go, his body warm and content. Tonight he'd give Leslie whatever he wanted.

"Well, look at you getting it on in public. I thought it was you." The sneering voice catapulted Oliver back into a dark place. He blinked as he looked up into the smarmy face of Gregori Golovin. He was flanked by the twins, Pierce and Payton, who, as usual, were simpering behind him.

"Greg. And acolytes." There had been a time when Greg's long platinum hair and brilliant green eyes, his lithe, limber body and tanned skin had been Oliver's everything. Now, his mind conjured only dark blue eyes and black hair when he thought of someone he cared about. "I can't say it's a pleasure to see any of you. Now could you just turn around and leave?"

Gregori snorted and hooked a chair over with his foot, then sat down next to Oliver. "Go fetch me a drink," he commanded to Pierce. "Payton, can you grab me some food before that greedy bunch of vultures eat it all? I want to talk to my boy Nicky on my own." The twins nodded and melted into the crowd behind them.

"I'm not Nicky anymore, Greg," Oliver said quietly. "I'm just plain Oliver."

"Oh, I know that," Gregori replied with a smirk. "You were washed up the minute you trashed your face. Booze and drugs will do that to you." He leaned closer and peered at Oliver's face. "Wow, they did a really bad job of patching you up. I can still those scars."

He reached out a hand to move Oliver's hair from his face and Oliver grabbed it tightly.

"You don't get to touch me," he snarled, his fingers gripping Gregori's wrist. "You don't have that right anymore."

"Oh but twinky boy does?" Gregori grinned nastily. "You seem to be slumming it now, Nicky. I guess that's all you're good for with a face like that."

Heat rushed through Oliver and he wanted to punch the smug face in front of him for those comments. He held back. This was a public place and the last thing he wanted was a lot of attention. Gregori no doubt knew that from the glint in his eyes that told him to bring it on.

"Fuck off," Oliver growled. "I'm over you, so piss off. Go find your toy boys to drill you a new one."

Gregori pulled out his phone. "I was watching you from the minute you walked in and I recognised you," he said dangerously. "So I had my boys follow that twink around and guess what they found? He doesn't just belong to you, Nicky. He has someone else on the side." He held up his phone and waggled it in front of Oliver, whose hands trembled under the table and breath seemed to be getting shorter. He didn't believe Gregori; it was all just a plot to rile him. So when Gregori laid his phone down on the table and there, in full HD colour, was the picture of Leslie kissing another man, a well built, hunky fellow, Oliver felt faint. The date stamp was clearly marked tonight, at ten-thirty pm when Leslie had been gone.

Gregori was watching him closely. "I wasn't lying, was I? He's a bit of a slag, leaving you here like that and then getting off with another guy."

Oliver leaned forward and poked Gregori hard in the chest. "Don't you call him that, you bastard. Leslie is no slag."

He had no doubt there had to be a reason for that picture. Perhaps it had been something innocent, something misconstrued. He'd have to ask him. Leslie wasn't the sort to do that to a man. That much Oliver knew.

Gregori shrugged his broad shoulders. "Well, pardon me. I suppose denial comes easy in your situation. Denial that you don't look like a monster. Denial that your *man*"—he spat the words out—"isn't off fucking someone else. Denial that you aren't a has-been porn star and drug addict who needed coke to get it up on set and make it through the day."

Oliver tried not to let the words get to him but he was shaking. He remembered the pain of the accident, the surgery, the skin grafts, the pain he'd faced with only Katie by his side. He remembered too well Gregori's sneering rejection. The withdrawal process had been painful and difficult. Although he hadn't been on the coke for too long, his addiction was bad enough that he'd suffered plenty through giving it up.

"So," Gregori drawled. "I just wanted to share that with you and tell you that honestly, you need to let it go. This guy isn't going to want you, *Nicky Starr*. He already has someone else anyway, someone who probably hasn't had half of London up his arse. You fucked up our relationship with your high morals and you'll do the same to this one sooner or later. You always do." He stood up. Oliver saw Pierce and Payton approaching the table with drink and food and Gregori waved them over.

"Guys, leave that here with our friend Nicky. He looks like he could use a drink. Probably the first time he's been out in public since his face was torn off. Disgusting, subjecting everyone else to it, too."

The twins laughed.

Even though Oliver knew no one could see the jagged scar, his hand still instinctively went to his face.

"Yeah, we saw 'his' guy over at the bar. He's luscious." One of the twins winked suggestively. Oliver had no idea which one it was; he'd never been able to tell them apart. "I wouldn't mind putting this between that tight arse and giving him one." The man grabbed his crotch and rocked his hips crudely.

Gregori laughed harshly. "I'd fuck him myself. Love to get inside that hot hole."

Oliver stood up, fists clenched. "I'm going to fucking kill you, Greg." He moved toward him and the men formed a flank together like a wall of Armani suits and gold jewellery. He didn't care if they beat him up. No one insulted Leslie like that.

"I wouldn't if I were you," Gregori said dangerously. "I've got someone at the bar keeping an eye on your little bit of fluff. You start something, he'll get hurt."

Oliver stared at the three men helplessly and unclenched his fists.

Gregori gave an unpleasant smile. "That's better." He flicked an imaginary piece of something off Oliver's collar, "I'd suggest you quit while you still can. Go back to your miserable, solitary life and be the man you were born to be. Nothing."

Oliver's despair flooded him but he tried not to let it show. He didn't think he was succeeding from the victorious grin on Gregori's face. Old insecurities and fears invaded his body and his mind like soldier ants on their way to a tasty feast. Gregori looked as if he'd just won the lottery, the smirk on his face growing wider with every beat of Oliver's bruised heart.

"So, why not sit down and wait for your boyfriend? Maybe you can ask him about the other guy when he comes back. The two of you can have a cosy little tête-à- tête and he can find out exactly how bloody pathetic you really are. Come on, you two."

Gregori moved off, his two shadows close behind him. Oliver stood there for a while, swaying on his feet, wanting to be sick. He had no idea how much time had passed until he felt a warm hand on his arm as an anxious familiar voice murmured in his ear.

"Are you all right, Oliver? You look as if you're going to faint." Leslie's strong hands helped him back to the table and he sat down, closing his eyes, wishing he was anywhere else but here. Leslie fussed around him as he handed him a glass of water.

"It's probably nerves," Leslie soothed. "All this activity and people after being a hermit is bound to give anyone a bit of anxiety. Here, drink this."

Oliver obediently drank the water, waiting for his racing heart to calm down. Leslie's blue eyes looked at him with concern.

"Feeling better? Sorry, I tried to get as back as soon as I could…"

The words left Oliver's mouth like vomit. "Someone said they saw you kissing another guy. Is this true?"

Leslie's face paled. "Oh my God, is that what got you all aflutter? It was just Frankie—he was drunk. I gave him a good slap, told him I was out of bounds. He apologised but not before he tried to kiss me. God, Oliver, I'm so sorry. It really didn't mean anything. Like I said, he'd had too much to drink and was a feeling a bit amorous." He sat down beside Oliver, placing a tentative hand on his.

Oliver passed a trembling hand over his forehead. "Who's Frankie?"

"He works at the building site next door to work. He's been trying to get me to go out with him for ages but I've been telling him no. Because I have you." His voice quailed. "I do have you, don't I?"

Oliver tried to process all the thoughts spiralling in his head. He rubbed his eyes tiredly. "I don't know. I can't think."

Leslie reached for his hand. "Frankie is just a friend. He's the son of the guy who owns the construction company. We see each other now and then when he goes out for a smoke, or pops in to say hi at work."

The kiss, Gregori's words, the knowledge of who Oliver had been and who he now was, the fact someone else wanted Leslie, someone who could probably offer him so much more…they all flooded his brain with images and sensations and he felt the familiar darkness creeping up.

"Look, Leslie, I don't feel so well. I'm going to call a taxi and go home and get some sleep. I need to be alone for a while, you know? This is all a bit much and I need to shut off for a bit." He stood up, hating the stricken look on his boyfriend's face, the pain in his eyes.

"Uhm, yes, okay. If that's what you need to do. Of course. Let me call you a cab…"

"No." Oliver's voice came out sterner than he'd meant it to and Leslie's eyes flickered. "I can do this myself. You get back to your party and celebrations and I'll call you tomorrow." He walked away, tears stinging his eyes, not wanting to see whatever devastation he was leaving behind. He needed to do this—leave and not look back before he lost it completely.

* * *

Leslie slumped down on a chair, his hands trembling, the numb feeling in his chest threatening to take over. What the fuck had happened tonight? One minute everything was going fantastically and they were well on their way to Oliver's house for a night of loving, and the next, his lover was walking away, alone, with a look on his face that left Leslie cold inside. Over a kiss? He wondered who'd told Oliver about it.

"Fuck you, Frankie," he muttered softly. "Why did you have to do that?"

In truth, he couldn't blame Frankie for this one. The look in Oliver's eyes, the despair on his face—that hadn't simply been from the kiss incident. Something else was going on, he was sure of it. Perhaps he had pushed Oliver too hard. Perhaps seeing all these beautiful people around him had pushed him over the edge.

"He looked so lost," Leslie whispered. "Like he has nothing. But he has me."

He knew he had fallen head over heels for Oliver Brown. The desire to shout out the words 'I love you' had taunted Leslie more than once, but he'd resisted. It was too soon, surely, he'd told himself, even when he knew it was the truth. He'd never felt about anyone the way he felt about Oliver.

And now it seemed his world had changed and all he could hope was that he'd get the chance to tell Oliver the words he'd been holding back. And the night had only just begun. In the distance, he saw Taylor frown and start walking toward him. The man's sixth sense was uncanny. Leslie could only watch with dread in his heart as his friend approached with a worried look as Leslie tried to hold the tears at bay.

## Chapter 14

Oliver paced up and down the lounge as he watched the street. He was on tenterhooks waiting for Leslie to get here. After he'd got home last night, he'd stripped off his clothes and fallen straight into bed. His sleep had been uneasy, troubled with thoughts and emotions that he didn't want to name. Finally he'd fallen asleep, after making the decision that was currently making his stomach grumble and cramp in anxiety.

The text he'd sent to Leslie this morning had been simple enough.

*Morning. Can you maybe come over later? I really need to see you.*

Leslie's reply text had come over within a minute of him sending his.

*Of course. Hope you're feeling better. I'll be there around midday. Got something to tell you too. xxoo*

He saw Leslie walking up the path, hugging his arms around his body. Oliver moved away from the window and waited for the doorbell. It sounded and he walked over and opened the door. Leslie stood there, impeccable as always in tight dark jeans, high-heeled boots and a deep blue turtleneck. He had a bright rainbow-coloured scarf draped around his neck. He looked a little uncertain.

"Hi. Come in." Oliver stood back, his heart hammering with apprehension and grief. He wanted to vomit the cereal he'd eaten this morning into the nearest receptacle. Instead he watched Leslie brush past him, a worried smile on his face.

"I was so pleased to get your text to come over. You worried me last night. The guys were worried, too. I said you'd had a bit of a panic attack and needed to go home." His look of concern made Oliver want to run and never come back. He didn't think he could bear to see the hurt on Leslie's face when he told him the news.

*It's the right thing to do*, he told himself. *Leslie deserves more than this. He's too damned good for the likes of someone like me. I'll just hold him back.*

"Sit down, Leslie. Please." He waved toward the sofa and Leslie looked at him curiously.

"Are you okay? You sound a bit strange." Leslie came toward Oliver, his intention to steal a hello kiss obvious. Oliver moved away and stood behind the couch. If Leslie kissed him, held him, he'd cave in and not do this. He needed to be strong for Leslie's sake.

His lover's face shadowed, and Oliver saw the realisation on it that whatever news he was about to be told, it wasn't good. Leslie's eyes widened, his face paled and he stared at Oliver like someone had just stolen his favourite teddy bear. His voice, when he spoke, was husky, uncertain.

"Oliver? What's going on?" His shoulders hunching over, Leslie gripped the top of the couch.

Oliver took a deep breath and broke his own heart. "I've been doing some thinking and this isn't working anymore for me."

Leslie's blue eyes darkened. "What isn't working for you, Oliver? Us? Is it because of that damn kiss from Frankie?" His fingers gripped the couch, his knuckles whitening. He swallowed and gazed at Oliver steadily.

Oliver nodded and wanted to crawl into a dark pit at the flash of pain that crossed Leslie's face. "No, I believe you on the kiss. I just don't think I'm ready for all this yet. I thought I was and I know this is coming as a bit of a surprise to you, but I don't want to lead you on anymore."

Leslie's tongue came out and wet his lips as he nodded. "I see. What happened between last night and today? Your text said you really needed to see me. I thought it was all okay…"

"Nothing happened. I just figured out what I wanted, that's all."

"And it isn't me." Leslie straightened up, and Oliver saw his hands were trembling. His eyes glistened. "What did I do? Did I do something wrong? I know I can come on too strong, but I can tone it down, I promise…"

Oliver's heart shattered into a million tiny shards that threatened to drive deep into his flesh and bleed him dry. Leslie's persona was exactly what made him love him so much. This man should never have to change who he was.

*Oh God, give me strength to do this.*

"No Leslie, it's not you at all. It's just this all went too far, too quickly, and I need space. And I don't want the pressure of being in a relationship while I figure out what I want to do."

*You need to find somebody who will worship you like I do, but without all the baggage. Not a washed up ex-drug addict porn star with a scarred face and a trunk full of insecurities. You deserve to shine, like the star you are.*

"Oh." Leslie's eyes shimmered and he swallowed again. "So that's it then? It's over?" His shoulders hunched, and his eyes sparkled with tears. Oliver watched as one trickled down and he ached to wipe it off his porcelain cheek.

"I'm sorry, Leslie. I didn't set out in this meaning to hurt you, but you know my background. You know what I've been doing the past two years and I need that solitude back. It's better that way."

Leslie shook his head. "What if I don't accept that? I don't want to break up, Oliver. I love you. That's what I wanted to tell you. I don't want to leave." His voice grew stronger as he stood up straight and glared at Oliver. One hand came up to fiercely brush the tear off his cheek. "When do I get a say in this? I'll give you time if that's what you need, plenty of it. Just please don't send me away. Please don't do this."

Oliver tried to keep the quake from his voice at the words *I love you*. They struck his heart with the ferocity of an arrow and left him mortally wounded. "I'm sorry. I've thought a lot about this and it's what I want. There's nothing you can say that will change my mind."

*You don't really love me, Leslie. You just think you do. Now, you have to leave, now.*

The tension in the air was palpable and when Leslie spoke again, his voice was tight and controlled. "Suit yourself, Oliver. I can see you've convinced yourself that this is what you want to do, so I guess I can't argue. I don't know what the hell is going on with you, but I don't think this is what you really want. "

*He knows me too well. He sees right inside me.*

Leslie moved toward the door, his slender frame taut and angry. "I'll leave then. When you come to your senses, call me. I'll be there, waiting. And if you don't call…" he shrugged. "Then I guess I'll know I was wrong about you and about everything I thought we had." He laughed harshly. "It wouldn't be the first time and it probably won't be the last. I guess I'm too damn trusting."

He reached the door and put his hand on the door handle. Oliver waited, ready to bolt to the bathroom and be ill the minute Leslie left.

His lover turned around and the despair on his face was more than Oliver could bear.

He stood firm. "Thanks for understanding, Leslie. I hope you find the right man to love you one day."

Leslie stared at him, his face flooded with pain. "I thought I already had," he said quietly. Then he opened the door and walked out of Oliver's house—out of his life.

Oliver had never felt so dark and despairing, even when he'd been in the hospital. His legs threatened to collapse and as Leslie shut the door behind him, Oliver sank to the floor and wept tears of blood and grief as his broken heart exploded.

## Chapter 15

Leslie burrowed down deeper into the covers and tried to ignore the persistent throb in his head from the alcohol he'd drunk the night before. He opened bleary eyes and peered at the clock. His heart pounded when he realised it was already eight-thirty am He was supposed to be at work.

"Shit. Fuck." He pushed back the covers, and sat up, wincing as his brain felt like it was smashed against the inside of his skull.

"I am never drinking tequila again," he vowed as he made his unsteady way to the shower. He thought he might still be a little bit drunk. "And I am definitely not doing karaoke with Eddie ever again. Who knew the man could sing like that?"

Last night his friends, worried at his depression over Oliver splitting up with him, and fed up of him wallowing in his flat for the past week and a half, had taken him to a karaoke bar in Soho, not far from Galileo's. They'd all four come by, threatened to knock the door down and then, when he opened it, made him shower, dress and come out with them.

He scowled as he got into the scalding shower. Getting on stage with Eddie, and hearing him belt out 'Mustang Sally' like a pro, complete with the gravelly voice, had left Leslie as envious as hell. He'd always wanted to be able to sing, but didn't really have the voice. Gideon's pride at his boyfriend's achievement had definitely promised dividends later and the gooey-eyed looks they thrown at each other had made Leslie sick with despair because he had lost Oliver and had no one anymore.

Well, except Frankie. Sort of. If Leslie chose to go down that road.

He and Frankie had been on a couple of non-dates *as friends*, as Leslie had told him firmly. They'd been to the movies, eaten pizza and had a few drinks together. As much as he enjoyed the ebullient Frankie's company, Leslie really wasn't ready for any sort of relationship now. The last one had taken it all out of him.

Last night Draven had been showing Taylor magic tricks and making him all *wow, look at you, you stud,* which again promised some late-night activity, and Leslie had got fed up with being the fifth wheel. He knew they didn't mean to be insensitive about his single status, but they just couldn't help themselves.

He'd finally left his friends singing 'Dancing Queen' on the stage and gone home to a bottle of his own tequila. *That* decision he was really regretting.

He smirked. At least he'd got something out of the evening. He'd videotaped the guys singing ABBA and already uploaded it to his YouTube account. Now *that* was a decision *they* might regret.

He got into work around nine-thirty, prepared to face his boss's ire. Surprisingly enough no one said anything to him and he thought he might have gotten away with it.

When he was summoned to Laverne's office around ten, he sighed. He knew it had been too good to be true. He knocked on his boss's door and heard her loud 'Enter.' When he went in, Laverne waved a hand toward the chair.

"Have a seat, sweetie."

Leslie's eyebrows lifted. Maybe the endearment meant he wasn't in trouble.

Laverne looked at him from beneath strong brows. "How are you doing?"

"In what way?" Leslie was puzzled.

Laverne sighed. "Leslie, since Oliver broke up with you, you've been a little distracted. Nothing affecting your work," she forestalled Leslie's panicked denial, "but I've noticed you're not your usual bubbly self. I know this is normal, of course, all things considered." She frowned as noise from the building site next door threatened to drown her out. "Those boys need to keep it down a bit. They've been really noisy today for some reason."

She leaned forward. "I've been concerned about you and just wanted to check in."

Leslie looked down at his shoes. "I'm okay," he muttered. "Getting over it."

In fact, nothing could be further from the truth. His heart was still raw from Oliver's rejection. Leslie had hoped that he would hear from him, and he hadn't been proud enough to keep from sending a few texts asking Oliver if they could talk. He'd gotten one terse text back.

*It's over. Please stop contacting me.*

After that, he'd fallen apart and realised that it really was over and Oliver didn't want him anymore. Taylor had been there to pick up the pieces, wipe up the tears that fell copiously from Leslie's eyes and tell him fiercely that he was going to go over to Oliver's and kick his arse. Leslie had managed to convince Taylor that Oliver wasn't to be touched, but he wasn't so sure about convincing Draven.

Taylor's man had got this gimlet-eyed look as if was about to take out a hit on someone. He'd gruffly patted Leslie's head like a puppy and told him that Oliver was a complete arsehole letting someone like Leslie get away, and that in his future there might be some *payback*.

Leslie had shivered at the way he'd said that and hastily asked Taylor to please tell Draven not to interfere. The last thing he wanted to read in the news that an ex-porn star recluse had been found beaten or tortured in his house.

"No you're not." Laverne stood up, focused Leslie back to the present, and came over to him, pulling him to his feet. "Come here. You need a hug."

Leslie was enveloped in strong arms and it was all he could do not to cry at such concern. Instead he closed his eyes, breathed in Laverne's perfume and revelled in the firmly muscled chest under which a strong heart beat. Laverne might be woman on the outside but underneath that person was all man.

Finally Laverne released him and watched with kind eyes. "You're a tough little bugger, Leslie. You'll get over this." She grinned. "Maybe it's time to take that sexy Frankie up on his offer. God knows if I was a bit younger, I'd want to tap that."

Leslie sniffed. "Maybe I will. He called me yesterday actually, asking me to go with him to a rock concert. As a date, not a friend. I might…"

There was a mighty roar outside and the building shuddered. Leslie yelled in panic and grasped Laverne's arm. "My God, what was that?"

Outside, there was the sound of people screaming and crying and both of them dashed over to the window. Leslie's throat clenched as he observed the carnage outside. The scaffolding from the renovations next door had crumbled to the ground, lying in the street in a tumble of concrete, wood and metal. People ran around, trying to get to the injured obviously trapped under the debris. In the distance already there was the sound of sirens.

"Oh, Christ." Laverne's face was white. "Leslie. Get all the staff rounded up to help." She moved away from the window. "Anybody who can render assistance should come downstairs and give us a hand to get those people out from under that wreckage. And if anyone mentions they can't because of bloody health and safety, tell them they're fired."

Leslie nodded frantically. He didn't really think you could fire people for observing the safety laws, but Laverne was a law unto herself. He followed her as she rushed from the room.

*What about Frankie?* he wondered helplessly. He might be buried under there, hurt, even dead. Leslie swallowed as he darted around the office mustering the Debussy troops.

"Please be okay, Frankie," he whispered to himself. "I need you to be safe."

\* \* \*

Oliver sat flicking the channels on his remote control. He didn't really see what he was looking at. His mind was still too crowded with blue eyes filled with devastation and a face that had etched itself into his painful memories. The words *I love you* still circled in his brain like hungry sharks, slashing at his thoughts, drawing blood.

*If it was the right thing to do, why do I feel like shit?*

For the thousandth time, he wondered what Leslie was doing now. Was he with Frankie, with a man who could laugh and take him places without falling apart? Had he moved on already, or was he too like Oliver, pitiable, useless, reduced to takeout food and alcohol to take the pain away? Oliver hoped not. That hadn't been his intention. One pathetic arsehole was enough.

He threw the remote down next to him on the couch, and pressed himself tighter into the corner of the cushions.

*Why?* he asked himself, second-guessing his decision to cut Leslie free. *Did you make the right decision? Or were you just overreacting to that bastard Gregori and his damning words about being a nothing, just a hole to fill? Did you just send away the best thing to ever happen to you?*

He stared at the television, seeing the pictures flash across it of some building or other that had collapsed but not really caring. It was only when he heard the words *London* and *Debussy's* that he started to pay attention. He frowned and picked up the remote to turn up the volume.

"To repeat, earlier this morning, building scaffolding collapsed in Diamond Street, Hackney." The presenter's voice was subdued. "At this moment it is not known how many people are injured, but we do know that there have been two fatalities." The camera focused on a scene far away and then zoomed in. "It has affected local businesses in the area, notably the fashion house, Debussy's, and well-known auctioneer Raymond Powell's. The local cafe below was also a popular gathering place for workers in the area. At this time it is not known whether any of these staff were involved in the accident."

Bile rushed up Oliver's throat. He could make out a hand covered by a tarpaulin. From underneath, he saw only the top of a head, a head covered in black hair just like Leslie's. He stood up, shaking, the blood rushing from his head, pooling in his stomach; his skin rose in goose bumps and he had to take deep breaths to centre himself.

"Oh my God, Leslie," he whispered, his heart clenching. The sick feeling in his stomach increased. His mind blanked out and for a moment, he couldn't breathe.

"The emergency services were on the scene quickly and the injured are still being moved to the local hospital. Rescue teams are attempting to locate people who may still be buried under the rubble." The presenter turned and waved at the scene behind her. "As you can see, they have help from many of the local businesses that have come out to assist the rescue team in moving the debris. At present, there is no explanation for the collapse but some of the construction crew have said it appeared to be a faulty building pillar that was weakened by recent drilling activity. I understand the reason for the tragedy still remains to be investigated and we will bring you more news as we have it."

The television reverted to the in-studio team on the news and Oliver stood, swaying slightly. A feeling of dread coursed through his body and he knew he had to get down there. Find out whether Leslie was safe. With trembling fingers, he dialled Leslie's mobile.

"Please answer," he prayed fervently. "Please, Leslie, answer."

The ringing tone in his ears mocked his distress and he cut the call off as it went to voicemail. He wasted no more time. He rushed to the bedroom, threw on jeans and a sweatshirt and ran out of the house. Flagging down a taxi and clambering in with instructions to take him to Diamond Street, he tried calling Leslie again. There was still no reply.

"You do know that place is a mess, right?" the taxi driver told him, catching his eye in the rear view mirror. "A bloody building collapsed. I might not be able to get you too close."

"That's fine," Oliver said distractedly as he called Leslie again. "Just get as close as you can. I have a friend there who might be hurt."

*Or worse.*

"A'right mate. I'll get you there. Hold on. This could be a bumpy ride." The vehicle swung out into the busy traffic and Oliver sat back, palms sweating, hands trembling, hoping to all the gods and fates in the universe that there was still time to make things right with the man he loved.

It took almost ninety minutes to even get close to the accident site. The distance was only about six miles but the traffic was horrendous. The driver, Emmett, kept up a running commentary about the vagaries of the London roads and transport system and more than once, Oliver thought he would get out and run the rest of the way. Emmett was always optimistic, saying they'd be there soon, but by the time they hit gridlock again not far away, Oliver was beside himself. There was still no reply from Leslie. The business phone was busy, and he hadn't anybody else's personal contact numbers.

When the taxi stopped once more behind a stream of exhaust-spewing, stationary traffic, Oliver could bear it no longer. He fumbled in his wallet for the money he owed and tucked it between the windows of the front of the cab.

"I have to get there," he said desperately as Emmett's eyes widened. "Thanks for the ride."

He checked; there were no bikes or motorcycles coming past, opened the door and leapt out into the street. His feet hit the pavement and he began running. A steady jog, nothing fast, but he knew that every step he took brought him closer to Leslie. Luckily

Oliver was fit; his own little home gym was paying dividends. His hair bounced and bobbed around his face as he ran but the state of his face and that fucking scar meant nothing, absolutely nothing compared to what might have happened. The only thing on his mind was saying sorry to a man with hair as black as coal and begging him to give him a second chance.

If he wasn't too late.

Finally, Oliver saw the crowd in the distance, and he sped up. The area looked as if it was still being cordoned off, and Oliver hoped he wouldn't be stopped by the rescue services or police. He thought grimly that there was no way in hell they were stopping him finding Leslie. He'd fight to the death if he had to.

Panting, he stopped on the outskirts of the carnage and stared around in horror. The quaint building of Debussy's appeared intact but the site next to it was a wreck. It was a low building, probably three storeys high and while most of it was still standing, the left-hand side was ripped open. Plaster and beams hung down, metal poles dangled thirty feet off the ground, and long wooden struts lay smashed to splinters on the pavement.

Men and women in high-visibility jackets, police and paramedics, surrounded the scene in well-organised chaos. Everywhere Oliver looked, there were people moving planks, struts and pieces of concrete. Several cars were dented and squashed and the glass front of the little coffee shop where Leslie often bought his coffee was smashed to shards.

Oliver ran over to the front entrance of Debussy's, chest heaving. The door was locked and he had no idea whether anyone still remained inside. He hoped that it was the case.

A woman standing smoking saw him pulling at the door. She shook her head. "Everyone's out helping," she told him. "The guys locked the door so they didn't get looted while they cleaned up. You know what some people are like." Her eyes conveyed disgust as such a scenario.

Oliver stared at her blankly. "Were there any casualties from this place, do you know?" he waved at Debussy's. "Anyone get hurt?"

She shrugged and took another drag of her cigarette. "Don't know."

He turned and moved forward as if in a dream, eyes anxiously searching for the form of his boyfriend. The area was taped off and people milled behind the barriers, watching the events unfold. No one stopped him as he slipped through the bollards across the street and pavements. They all seemed to be occupied in the area outside the coffee shop. He'd been lucky.

Oliver moved through the frenetic activity. "Leslie," he shouted. "Leslie Scott!" His shouts brought him no response other than agonised glances as people spattered with blood and dust moved around the site. Once or twice he thought he saw the slim form of his lover and his heart raced in anticipation, but when he got there, he was disappointed.

He got closer to the coffee shop and saw a pile of planks and metal beams with half a dozen people standing around the heap. Desperately he grasped the nearest person, a broad-shouldered man coated in dust.

"Have you seen a man called Leslie? Slim, black hair, blue eyes? I really need to find him."

"Mate." The man's voice was quiet. "He's over there." He motioned to the rubble and Oliver's whole being went cold. The man realised his mistake and his eyes widened.

"No, *he's* okay. It's his friend…" The man's voice tailed off. "He won't leave him. We're waiting for the paramedics; they should be here anytime soon."

Oliver nodded a wordless *thank you*, his eyes brimming with tears of relief at the realisation that Leslie was all right. He moved around the waist-high pile and lost his breath when he saw him.

Leslie sat cradling a man in his arms, a man whose face was waxen-white, eyes closed and so full of blood Oliver thought he couldn't possibly be alive. Leslie was hunched over the still form, stroking the man's face, murmuring something. His lover looked like a dark phoenix about to rise from the ashes. His white dress shirt was ripped and bloody, his hands scraped and bleeding. Leslie's dark hair was covered with dust and pieces of plaster. He looked up and spoke to the man beside Oliver, not even seeming to recognise he was there.

"Dasher, where are those paramedics? Frankie's really cold."

The big man Oliver had spoken to moved forward. "They're on their way over, Leslie. I can see them. Just a couple of minutes, little 'un."

"But he doesn't have minutes," Leslie's agonised whisper tore at Oliver's heart. "He's dying, Dash. And we haven't even had that first date yet."

Oliver quelled the fear those words caused. There were more important things to think about right now. He needed to be there for Leslie.

"Leslie, sweetheart? It's Oliver."

Leslie's eyes flickered, looking dazed. "Oliver?"

"Yes, love. I'm here." He clambered over the boards and knelt down beside both men. "I heard about the accident and I rushed over. God, I was so worried about you."

The blank stare he got back in return scared him.

"He won't wake up," Leslie whispered, looking down at the man in his arms. "I've been talking to him but he won't open his eyes." His voice cut off as he choked up.

Oliver reached over and laid his fingers against the Frankie's throat, trying to track down a pulse. He smiled in relief as his fingers found what he was looking for.

"He's alive. Faint, but it's there." He looked up as two people, the paramedics, pushed their way through with a stretcher and crouched down beside them. The man and woman looked tired and drawn but the woman smiled softly at Leslie as they got to work.

"Hi, there. We're going to try and help your friend, okay? Do you think you could move a bit so I can get in, see what needs doing?"

Leslie stared at them unseeingly and Oliver wrapped his arms around him and tried to move him away. "Let's let them see to Frankie, shall we? If we move over here, they'll have room to work. Come on."

He helped Leslie up with a little resistance, and they stood and watched as the paramedics worked on the unconscious man. Leslie was trembling and cold and Oliver thought he might be in shock. He enfolded Leslie into his chest with a feeling that this was exactly where he should be. He was never letting go of him again, if Leslie took him back. From the sound of it, he might already be too late to make amends.

"I was so bloody scared, Leslie," he murmured into his ear. "I saw someone covered up in a bag and he looked like you. I died inside."

Leslie said nothing, but his heart beat steadily against Oliver's chest, his cheek against Oliver's shoulder, as he watched the paramedics with Frankie. The man Leslie had called Dasher was looking at him with a challenging look and he moved over to them.

"You're the git who broke up with him?" he said quietly.

Oliver couldn't deny it. "Yes, I'm that git."

Dasher nodded. "Broke his heart, you did. I'm glad to see that you're here for him now, but don't ever fucking do that again." His tone was threatening, but conversational. Leslie shifted in Oliver's arms.

Oliver nodded. "I won't." He kissed the top of Leslie's head. "But now's not the time to talk about it."

Dasher's eyes narrowed. "You got that right. This is a fucking disaster." He squinted and looked around. "I'm going to go see if I can help some more. You look after him, you hear? Or I'll be coming after you." He started to move away but was stopped as the paramedics moved across his path bearing the stretcher with Frankie on it.

Leslie pulled away from Oliver and walked toward them. "I want to go with him," he murmured softly. "I need to be there with him when he wakes up."

The paramedic looked a bit uncertain. "Are you his boyfriend or family perhaps?" she asked as she bit her lip worriedly.

"I'm his friend. And I've been sitting with him there talking to him and making sure he stays alive until you got here." Leslie's voice was pure steel. "And I *am* going in that ambulance."

Dasher snorted. "*There's* my boy." He turned to the paramedics. "I'd really suggest you let him go with you unless you want a strop. And he's right. He's the one who kept that young 'un alive, and was there for him. He deserves to be with him."

The male paramedic nodded curtly. "Come on, then. We need to get him in the ambulance." They walked away and Leslie moved to follow them. Oliver touched his arm and Leslie looked at him.

"I'll see you at the hospital," Oliver said. "Is that okay?"

Leslie's blue eyes regarded him evenly. "I'd rather you didn't. Frankie needs me right now and I don't have time for anything else. I'll call you." He walked after the paramedics and Oliver watched him go with a sense of helplessness and dread.

Dasher gave him a sympathetic glance. "Best leave him be at the moment," he advised gently. "He's got enough to think about without wondering what the ex is doing here when he wanted nothing more to do with him."

Those blunt words stabbed Oliver in the heart and he nodded as he swallowed the lump in his throat. "I know. It's just hard seeing him so upset, you know? I just want to be there for him." His voice trembled. "And I fucked up so badly and I don't know if I can get him back now."

"That's a tale for later, my boy." Dasher looked around. "Right now, we could use your help cleaning up. You in?"

Oliver nodded. "Of course. Just tell me what you want me to do."

Later that night when he lay in bed, his muscles stiff and sore, chest aching and wondering how Leslie was doing, Oliver closed his eyes and sent into the ether of the universe both heartfelt thanks that Leslie was safe and a desperate plea that he still had a chance to win Leslie back. This event had opened his eyes once again to the fact life was fleeting and you had to make the most of every minute while you could, and stop feeling sorry for yourself.

*I promise I'll do better this time. I'll be the best boyfriend ever. Just love me still, Leslie. That's all I'm asking.*

## Chapter 16

Eddie Tripp nudged Leslie on the shoulder and smiled at him from beneath untidy red locks of hair that spilled over his forehead. "Come on, Leslie," he shouted over the clamour of the stage and the fans surrounding it. "At least look as if you're having fun. You're at a Killers concert, for God's sake." He waved his hands over his head and sang along to the lyrics blaring out of the speakers all over the park.

Leslie sighed heavily and looked around the crowded venue. It was filled with happy people for the most part, a few drunks, stoners, and in the corner one man was stark naked and being escorted away by security staff. Even that sight did nothing to lift Leslie's darkened spirits.

In the two weeks since the construction accident, he'd seen Frankie through his surgery to repair multiple broken bones and lacerations, hugged him close when he had a bad day. Frankie was now back home in Suffolk with his parents, who were taking care of him until he was fully recovered. Leslie had also tried to forget the memory of Oliver's stark white face at the accident site. The sight of him standing there shocked and scared had made Leslie's heart beat faster despite his own panic at seeing Frankie injured. In the middle of calamity, being in Oliver's strong, warm arms had been heaven.

But he couldn't forget that Oliver had pushed him away. That Leslie had had his tender heart well and truly stomped on and then ground into the dirt. He'd said *I love you* to Oliver and it had counted for nothing. He didn't think he could go through that pain again.

In the days following his trip to the hospital with his friend, Oliver had texted him simply asking if they could talk. Leslie had texted back, telling him thanks for being there, but asked him to give him some more time.

Oliver had texted back one simple sentence.
*I'll wait. Call me when you're ready.*

Leslie's eyes had misted up reading that, but his resolve to take things slowly was at the forefront of his mind. He wanted Oliver back so badly it was all he thought about, but he wasn't sure he was ready to face him yet. He sighed again and decided his bladder definitely needed respite.

He tapped Eddie on the shoulder. "I'm going to the loo, Edster. At least," he looked doubtfully at the Portaloo about a hundred people away, "I'm going to try get there. Send out the Mounties if I don't come back in a while, will you?"

Eddie nodded and danced around to the music. Leslie rolled his eyes. His friend had a real thing for the band, and Brandon Flowers in particular. Although, who wouldn't have a thing for him, Leslie mused. The man was drop-dead sexy. He battled his way through screaming women, men and kids; his bladder about to shed its load and he fervently hoped he got there in time.

When he eventually arrived at the rather foul-smelling Portaloo, he almost decided not to go through with it. He looked around furtively. Maybe there was a spot he could just whip it out and no one would see. One grey-haired granny woman (really, at a Killers Concert? It just went to show that appearances could be deceiving— or perhaps it was Brandon Flowers' granny) gave him the evil eye as if she knew he was about to try to pee in public and he scowled at her.

"I hope you're not going to do what I think you are," she shouted at him across half a dozen dancing, waving, screaming people.

"Wouldn't dream of it," he called back and with a hidden snarl he made his way into the loo. It was as bad as he thought it would be and as he took out his aching dick and pissed into the grey, black-smeared urinal, (he didn't want to even imagine what that stuff was) he closed his eyes and pretended he was in the Ritz Hotel, aiming his pecker at a beautiful, porcelain vault, ready and waiting to catch the stream of his golden pee as it flowed effortlessly into its waiting mouth. When he opened his eyes and shook his dick, using some scrunched-up toilet paper to dry himself off, reality hit him and he shuddered.

"Ughh. This is just *so* not cool," he muttered as he tucked himself away and zipped up his Calvin Kleins. "Why do I let Eddie drag me to these bloody concerts? He knows I hate this public toilet stuff."

He knew the answer. His friends were once again trying to take his mind off Oliver. He wished his mind could take *itself* off his ex-lover.

As he left the Portaloo and stepped gingerly down the rickety stairs, drying his hands on his pants, someone gripped his shoulder. He turned, half defensively because who knew what tossers hung around public toilets at rock concerts, and his jaw dropped when he saw the shining blond hair of a person he now considered his archenemy. Gregori Golovin stood before him, a smirk on his face and eyes so dilated and black Leslie knew he was on something.

"I was right the first time," Leslie muttered to himself. "It *is* a tosser."

Gregori stared at him blearily and Leslie looked at the hand still on his shoulder.

"Do you want to remove that?" he said as loudly as he could. "It doesn't belong there." He looked around. "And where's your entourage? I though you always travelled with a pair of twats." He felt brave enough to chance being bold seeing the condition of the man standing before him. Leslie knew some moves. He'd watched Bruce Lee.

"I thought it was you," slurred Gregori. "Pretty boy, with the nice, tight arse. I told Nicky I wouldn't mind fucking it."

Leslie frowned.

*When had Oliver seen Gregori? While they'd been apart? And they'd talked about fucking his arse?*

His stomach lurched uncomfortably at the thought Oliver might have gone back to Gregori since they'd split up. The next words put his mind at ease a little but gave him something else to think about.

"You know, at that fancy fashion party you were both at, the one with all the naked guys," drawled Gregori. "I had a little chat with him. Told him a few home truths, showed him the picture of you getting off with your muscle man." He belched and Leslie stepped back, fearing he might be vomited on from the state of the other man's foul breath.

His heart was beating faster with every word spewing out of Gregori's mouth.

*All this had happened the night before he broke up with me.*

"What did you say to him?" Leslie demanded fiercely. Hope flared in his chest that perhaps now he might understand what made Oliver send him away.

Gregor grinned and swayed. "Told him he was an ugly loser, and that you were off kissing other guys anyway, so he wasn't going to keep you."

A light bulb went on in Leslie's head. "What else did you tell him?" His temper sparked at the look of greedy satisfaction in Gregori's eyes.

"Just the usual truths. That he's a worthless prat that didn't deserve to have anything good in his life." He squinted at Leslie. "You do know he got me kicked out of the best gig I ever had, yeah? Just for giving some kids what they needed." His face twisted into a snarl. "He turned the whole crew against me. They thought I was shit. I'll never forgive him for that. Fucking Nicky Starr, always more popular than me and I could never figure out why."

He took a step toward Leslie, reaching out a hand. "He looked so fucking happy with you. I had to teach him a lesson. Told him no one would want an ex-drug addict porn star who'd screwed half of London. You should have seen the look on that fucked-up face of his. It was priceless."

Leslie's blood was boiling. He wanted to punch this useless, interfering piece of shit in the face. This cruel, foul arsehole who took pleasure in beating Oliver down.

Finally, Leslie understood why Oliver had broken up with him. While part of him was furious at Oliver's lack of self-esteem and for letting Gregori prey on his insecurities to the point they got the better of him, the other part rejoiced because it all made perfect sense. Oliver did want him. He just didn't think he deserved him.

Well, Leslie was going to show Oliver just how wrong he was. After dealing with the prick in front of him who'd ruined Oliver's life.

He looked around, seeing a clear plastic cup of what looked like white wine perched on the bottom rung of the Portaloo next door. He pushed a startled Gregori out of the way, picked up the glass and flung the contents into Gregori's face. Leslie grinned in satisfaction at seeing the man howl and step back, falling over the stairs and landing flat on his arse.

"You little bitch. You just threw piss at me," Gregori screamed, spittle and what Leslie now knew to be urine bubbling on his lips.

"Oh, was that what it was? Sorry. My bad." Leslie was enjoying this. "You deserved to be pissed on, arsehole. If I hadn't already gone and drained the lizard, I'd piss on you myself. I have a message for you, you nasty piece of shit. Stay away from my boyfriend and stay away from me. Because I know a man who would enjoy killing you quietly and they'd never find your body. Right. I bet he'd just love to take you on."

Leslie wasn't sure Taylor would appreciate him pimping Draven out as a hired killer, but hey, that's what friends were for.

Gregori's eyes widened and he looked a little scared. Leslie smirked. The man was a bully and when you stood up to bullies, they tended to back off. He sniffed and turned away, hearing Gregori's curses and threats to ram something up his arse that wasn't his boyfriend's dick.

Leslie felt quite pleased with the turn of events. He looked at his watch. Ten p.m. Still time to leave the concert and get to Oliver's to confront the arsehole. He debated sending Eddie a text to tell him he was leaving then sighed. Eddie wouldn't hear it above the noise and he was probably belting out the 'Human' lyrics, the song now playing on stage. It was his favourite tune by the band.

Leslie made his way through the crowd, a little worried that he might not find his friend in the throng of people dancing about. Finally, after what seemed a trek through an Amazon jungle filled with dangerous dancing beasts and arms waving like tree trunks out to get him, he saw Eddie's red hair above the crowd. He heaved a thankful breath and latched onto Eddie.

Eddie turned, his eyes shining. "Isn't this great?" he yelled. "They are so radical, I love these guys."

"Yeah, they are," Leslie agreed. "Listen Eddie, I'm going to make a move. I need to see Oliver."

Eddie's mouth dropped. "Really? You need to do this now?" He cast a yearning glance back at the stage. "Can we just wait until the song finishes? I…"

Leslie laid a finger on his lips. He was warmed at the thought that without question Eddie would come with him. "No, Eddie, this is for me to do alone. You stay here and enjoy the rest of the show. I'm a big boy. I can make it on my own."

Eddie looked uncertain. "Are you sure, I can come with you if you need me..." He threw another pensive glance back at the stage.

Leslie leaned in and kissed his cheek. "I'm sure. Stay. Enjoy."

Eddie nodded. "Okay. Text me later, let me know you get there okay. I'll keep checking my phone." His eyes softened. "Did Oliver call you, or you him, is that what this is all about?"

Leslie shook his head. "No, let's just say I met someone who helped me put things in perspective. And now I really need to talk to Oliver."

"Okay. Remember to text me."

"I will. Enjoy the rest of the gig." Leslie kissed Eddie's cheek again softly then turned and made his way for the third time back through the throng, fighting to break through to the entrance, which seemed miles away.

His mind raced as he pummelled and pushed people out of his way. He knew the minute Oliver opened his door, and he saw his beloved face, that all the carefully planned words he'd rehearsed would disappear from his head like dissipating fog. But it gave him focus and quelled the feeling of apprehension in his belly that perhaps he was wrong after all.

\* \* \*

Leslie reached Oliver's house an hour and a half later. It had taken him ages to get out of the frenetic stadium then catch a tube to Oliver's. Now he stood on the doorstep, seeing no lights on and wondered whether he was doing the right thing. What if Oliver was sleeping? What if—and his heart lurched—God forbid, he had someone there? Maxwell perhaps, back from a flight and making a quick pit stop?

"You'll only find out one way, Leslie," he muttered and gritted his teeth as he rang the bell. The chime rang inside and he waited. The chill of the late-night air made him shiver and he wrapped his twill bomber jacket tightly around his body. An owl hooted somewhere and he started.

"Come on, Oliver, one way or another, you have to be here." He rang the bell again and after the final chime had dwindled, he heard someone at the door. He stared into the peephole, hoping his fierce stare conveyed to whoever might be behind the door that he meant business.

When the door swung open, he heaved a sigh of relief. Oliver stood there, clad in black joggers hanging low on his hips, hair tousled, face pale and drawn, eyes hooded in sleep. Leslie's cock stirred just at the sight of him.

*Thank God. I thought it was broken.*

"Leslie? Is everything all right? What are you doing here?"

Leslie pushed past him and let himself in. "I was in the neighbourhood and thought I'd stop by."

Oliver's face was the picture of confusion. "You were in the neighbourhood? What for?"

Leslie's insides jellied and his hands shook but he jutted his chin out and stared at Oliver in defiance as his ex-boyfriend (*soon to be not ex*, he hoped) shut the door. The words that came out definitely hadn't been the ones he'd rehearsed.

"There was this guy I know who decided to do something really fucking stupid because he felt he didn't deserve the best thing that ever happened to him because some ex- boyfriend plonker fed him a load of shit about himself. So I thought I'd come run that past him, see how he felt about it all?"

Oliver's eyes grew wide as Leslie unzipped his jacket, threw it carelessly on the hall table then sauntered though to the lounge, hoping he gave an air of aplomb that he certainly didn't feel. He heard something muttered behind him as he sat down on the couch, swung his legs up to settle comfortably and regarded Oliver.

"I'm sorry it's so late, but I was out at a rock concert. I met a friend of yours there who told me a few things, so I wanted to talk to you about them."

"What friend?" Oliver moved over to the couch and sat down gingerly on the arm. He drew his arms across his chest defensively.

"Gregori Golovin."

Oliver leapt up, his face twisting into a snarl. "That bastard. Did he hurt you? Because if he so much as touched you, or even breathed on you, I am going to break him apart bone by bone."

Leslie's attempt to be a bad boy wore off at the look of fear and hatred in Oliver's eyes. And the fact Oliver still cared enough to kill somebody for him.

"No, he didn't hurt me. It was the other way around, actually. I threw pee at him and he wasn't very pleased about it."

"He…you what?" Oliver passed a hand over his eyes. "Hell, Leslie, it's late, you woke me up, I'm really not sure why you're here so could you please tell me what's going on?"

Leslie wasn't feeling as confident as he'd been. "Okay. Here's the short version. Did you break up with me because you didn't think you deserved me and you thought I could do better?" Oliver's hitch in breath told him he'd hit the mark. "I mean… I know Gregori said some cruel stuff to you. He told me what he said. What I want to know, is anything you said to me the night we broke up true? About not wanting me anymore? Or was it just you being all noble and letting me go so I could find someone you thought was better?"

Oliver's shoulders slumped and his hands moved to his hair and ran through it absently. Leslie stood up and moved over to him, standing in front and looking into his hazel eyes. He ached to touch him, but he wasn't sure yet if he should.

"I know you care about me or you wouldn't have come down to the accident site, or sent me that text telling me you'd wait. But I have to know." He swallowed. "Do you still want me around?"

"Oh, baby." Oliver's voice was just a whisper, his voice broken. "I never stopped wanting you. I love you so damn much. Every quirky, beautiful, loving, warm, incredible bit of you."

Leslie hadn't realised he'd been holding his breath and he exhaled in a rush of warm air. Oliver's eyes closed and he seemed to breathe it in.

*Oliver loved him.*

"Then why…?" His fingers reached out and stroked Oliver's jawline, relishing the feel of the man's skin on his fingertips. Oliver's eyes held his and for a minute neither of them seemed able to breathe.

With a soft cry, Oliver pulled Leslie into him, his arms tightening, and when their lips found each other's, Leslie sighed and surrendered to the warm, male scent of sweat, shower gel and a desperate mouth seeking his. He'd missed Oliver's unique taste and fragrance and this was heaven.

When Oliver's hungry mouth pulled away, Leslie groaned and pulled it back.

Oliver chuckled. "Steady on. My dick's already thinking it's Christmas and I don't want to rush this. I need to apologise to you first."

"Don't care," Leslie moaned. "Just take me to bed, please. I missed you."

Oliver shook his head and plucked Leslie's hands out of the inside of his joggers. Leslie growled at the loss of the warm, velvety skin he'd been about to grasp.

"Oliver, I swear, I am going to self-combust if you don't do something to me. I've been a damn monk since you left and I'm really horny."

Oliver laid his forehead against Leslie's and stilled his eager hands.

"You've not been with anyone?" His voice was wondrous.

Leslie scowled. "Well, no. Duh. I was too busy getting over you, and I didn't want anyone else. I had my chances, I can tell you. There was Frankie, before he got all busted up, bless him. And I did have an offer from one of the guys at the karaoke evening we went to, but he was a bit skanky. He kept showing me all of his Grindr profile and it was just PPP… prick after prick pic." He warmed to his subject. "Oh, and there was a guy Tay introduced me to who was pretty cute looking, but he lived with his aunt and all he could talk about was these damn birds she bred. Honestly, I think I know everything there is to know about Belgian canaries. I didn't even know canaries came from other countries, I thought they were just canaries..."

He stopped as Oliver's body was shaking and he was making a strange noise. He peered at him anxiously. "Are you okay?"

Oliver looked up and Leslie's heart warmed to see the smile on his face, that soft twist of lips he'd missed seeing, and the eyes that shone with tears as he laughed silently.

"Oh, God," Oliver spluttered. "How the hell could I have gone so long without that crazy mouth of yours? You are unique, Leslie Tiberius Scott. The most incredibly beautiful and amazing person in the whole world."

Leslie stilled. "Then why did you send me away?"

Oliver framed his face in warm hands and nudged his nose gently. "Because I was an idiot. Because Gregori told me I didn't deserve anything good in my life and I believed him. I listened to my own insecurities instead of my heart."

He led Leslie over to the couch, sat down and pulled him into his lap. Leslie settled against him with a happy sigh and wriggled his arse against Oliver's hardened dick.

*I don't think it will be too long now and we'll be doing the horizontal mamba. Or maybe the vertical. I'm sure I saw a cowboy hat in Oliver's bedroom sometime…yee-haw.*

"I wanted you to do better for yourself." Oliver moved underneath him, trying to get comfortable and Leslie smirked. "Not be stuck with some guy who was still busy trying to make a life, get back into the world outside. You shine so brightly. I didn't want to be that guy dragging you down."

Leslie kissed his chin. "Well, you were an idiot. Just saying." He nibbled at Oliver's earlobe. "I like shining with you."

Oliver's face shadowed. "God, when I thought I might have lost you that day, nothing else mattered than making sure you weren't hurt. I realised nothing else mattered other than telling you I loved you."

"Message received and understood. I love you, too. Are we going to put this behind us now though? I really don't want anyone else." He laughed softly. "It just means training someone all over again."

Oliver nodded. "If it's okay, I'd like to start over."

Leslie slid his hands across Oliver's bare chest, seeing him shiver and his eyes darken. "Good. Now can we go to bed and fuck each other please? Tonight, though I'm going to drive. Want to be inside you."

He could tell Oliver really liked that idea by the way his cock jumped under Leslie's backside. In their previous sex life, Leslie preferred being the passenger, as he called it, but tonight—tonight he just need to make Oliver his. Then, he hoped everything would be all right and he'd have his boyfriend back.

\* \* \*

Seeing Leslie's hopeful face, Oliver knew he was a lucky man—lucky enough to have him back and to have been given this second chance. He desperately didn't want to mess it up.

"This time we are doing this in the bedroom," Leslie muttered as he propelled him toward his room. "I want a soft bed, mood lighting and ambience for this session."

Oliver snorted in laughter as Leslie pushed him inside and onto the bed. "I'm okay with that. My couch and that damn kitchen counter have never seen so much action."

He thought he and Leslie had probably christened every surface in the house, including the dining room table and the gym bench he used. That had been quite a notable event, including handcuffs and a lot of body contortions.

Leslie crawled on top of him and straddled his hips. He ground his backside against Oliver's groin as he smiled down at him and ran his fingers across his chest. His nipples hardened in response and his butt cheeks clenched as he anticipated Leslie between them.

Oliver groaned softly. "You're asking for trouble doing that," he whispered huskily. "I might fuck you before you get a chance to do me. So be careful what you wish for."

Leslie wiggled and puffed a soft breath on Oliver's face, making his nose twitch. "Just do as you're told," he warned, with a mock glower. Oliver thought his lover had never looked more bewitching and sexy than perched above him, blue eyes staring at him with avarice and need.

Immersed in a rush of love, Oliver felt warmth flush his veins and flesh with the knowledge this man was still his. He lost his breath and the room tilted in a strange kaleidoscope of colour. Reaching up, he pulled Leslie fiercely down on top of him, arms closing around his slim body in a loving vise.

"I'm glad you're here," he managed in a choked voice. "You mean the world to me, and I'm sorry I hurt you. I love you so much."

Leslie's mouth tickled his neck as he lay supine. "I know," he whispered. His tongue licked a sweet trail down the skin of Oliver's throat. "Now let me take care of you."

He sat up and pulled his shirt over his head and his smooth, lithe body was revealed, a sublime being, all planes, grooves and beauty. The front of his jeans jutted out with the rigid cock hidden inside and he smiled slyly as he began to unbutton his jeans teasingly.

"You want me inside you, Oliver? Deep inside, touching you, coming in you?" He licked his lips lasciviously and Oliver's groin burned with the fire of a thousand flames. Leslie stood up in one fluid movement and took off his jeans. Oliver gasped in awe at the sight of him in an emerald green thong, cock bulging against the silky material. Leslie turned around and presented his tight backside to Oliver. Two beautifully rounded and flawless cheeks bisected by a string that led to where Oliver wanted to be right now. Leslie waggled his arse at him.

"My turn with yours first. Then you can have this one."

Oliver couldn't speak. He watched as his lover slid the thong off his arse, down his legs then turned and knelt back down across him.

"Now to get rid of these," he murmured as he motioned for Oliver to lift his bottom and pulled the joggers off. Oliver's cock sprung up, wet, hot and aching, and Leslie's eyes dilated at the sight.

"God, I missed that," he whispered, then proceeded to wrap his mouth around the soft, velvety, swollen skin of it so tightly Oliver's hips left the bed and he cried out with the pleasure of it.

Leslie's hot, wet mouth circled, licked, sucked and teased, his hands resting on Oliver's thighs as he took him to a place in his head and body he'd not thought he'd find again. His hands clenched at the bed sheets, his legs shivered with the sensations running through his body and his vision ebbed and flowed as his lover gave him the blow job to surpass all others. He heard his own panting, his entreaties to Leslie to keep going, his garbled expletives and sobs as he spurred his boyfriend on.

Somewhere in the deep recesses of his brain, Oliver acknowledged this lust was caused by his celibacy since Leslie had been gone, having only his right hand and a vibrator to release the pent-up frustration he'd felt. The other sensation, one of being where he was supposed to be, in Leslie's mouth, his arms, his life, was the one trumping the horniness. It just felt so right.

He shuddered as he climaxed, his loud cry of satisfaction echoing in the bedroom as he shot his load into Leslie's waiting and greedy mouth, the rush seeming never to end. He was drained, sated, and as Leslie crept up his body to find his lips and kiss him with a hunger that promised even more, Oliver tasted himself, and the residue of his own fluids in Leslie's mouth.

"Lift your legs up, honey," Leslie murmured. "I need in you so badly."

He did as he was told and gasped when fingers breached him, already sticky with lube—*and when had Leslie done that?* Probably when he'd been passed out with the force of his orgasm. Oliver pushed his hole up to those questing fingers, desperate to impale himself deeper.

Leslie chuckled. "Easy, you greedy bugger. Let me do this properly."

Oliver closed his eyes and relished the fullness in his arse. Then he heard the rip of a foil packet.

"Leslie," he groaned, "Do we need a condom? I want to feel you inside me just as you are. You know my test results already. And I haven't been with anyone else since you left."

He and Leslie had already shared their results with each other before the breakup. They'd been debating whether to lose the condoms at that stage.

Leslie stilled. "I haven't either, but are you sure?"

Oliver traced Leslie's cheek tenderly. "Yes, love. I'm sure. I want this."

Leslie's smile lit up Oliver's world and as he pushed inside, their eyes met and Oliver was lost. The heat of Leslie's cock in his arse, the feeling of being taken, possessed so completely by him threatened to undo him.

Leslie's sighs and whispered endearments as he made love to Oliver and owned his body were the perfect soundtrack to what Oliver was feeling. It was their own personal romance film, the culmination of years of loneliness, insecurity and pain being transformed by the love of one man, a man who truly wanted him. Oliver smiled up at Leslie as the movie played out to its picture-perfect ending. There may still be a few trials ahead, but with Leslie by his side, he'd face them. The alternative wasn't an option.

When he felt the warmth of Leslie's semen inside him, the multiple '*Love yous,*' he sighed as he climaxed, and with the feel of skin against his as his lover collapsed on top of him, Oliver finally felt at peace.

They lay together afterward, half dozing, Leslie curled into Oliver's arms, head on his shoulder.

"So…" Oliver had been dying to ask but hadn't wanted to disturb their post-coital bliss until then. "How the hell did you manage to throw piss at Greg?"

Leslie giggled and Oliver was enchanted. "I didn't know it was pee," he retorted. "I thought it was wine someone had left on the step." He shrugged. "Turned out I was wrong."

Oliver spluttered with laughter. "God, he must have been mad." He stroked his lover's arm idly. "Still, things could have gotten nasty. That night of the fashion show, he threatened to hurt you if I hit him. I had to back off because that *so* wasn't happening."

"He was pretty drunk and drugged up, so not much of a threat." Leslie threw his leg over Oliver's as he got comfy. "And I know some karate, too. I'm not just a pretty face." He huffed indignantly and Oliver wanted to kiss him senseless for being so damned cute.

Leslie carried on. "Plus he was spilling the beans about what he'd said to you that night and I just had this feeling, I knew why you did what you did…."

Oliver kissed his dark head. "Thank God you had that feeling. Or we might not be here now." He hesitated. "I was going to call you again, I was going out of my mind, but I wanted to give you space."

"I suppose you could say Gregori Golovin did us a favour then," Leslie said sleepily, His eyes were half shut, lashes dark against his pale cheeks.

Oliver grinned happily in the darkness. "Yes, I think we can safely say for once in his miserable life, he did something right. I'm going to make sure I keep you by my side, Leslie Tiberius Scott. Right where you belong."

Soft lips brushed his side. "I like the sound of that. Now can we go to sleep please?" his boyfriend grumbled, giving him the stink eye. "I'm tuckered out and I need my beauty sleep." He frowned. "Although I have this feeling I should have done something and I haven't…"

"You couldn't be more beautiful," Oliver murmured softly as Leslie smiled at those words and closed his eyes again. "And whatever it is, it'll come to you. It couldn't have been that important. Sweet dreams."

Sleep wasn't long in claiming Oliver, and as he sank into the welcoming darkness, he wrapped the man in his arms in a protective embrace and gave thanks to the universe for bringing him back.

\* \* \*

In the middle of the night, rousing when Oliver's arm knocked him in the nose as he turned over, Leslie awoke with a start and the little thing that had been in the back of his mind niggling him as he'd fallen asleep came to the surface. "Shit. I forgot to text Eddie and tell him I got here safely. Hell, he's going to be pissed off."

He looked over at his sleeping lover, taking care not to wake him as he reached over to the bedside table and picked up his phone which lay charging. It read 3.12 am. He groaned softly.

"Four missed calls and half a dozen texts. Crap." He scrolled down, angling the phone away so the light didn't disturb Oliver and read the texts. It looked like Taylor and Eddie had worked in tandem in giving him hell.

Eddie: 11.30 pm. *You didn't text. Did you get to Oliver's okay?*
Eddie: 00.30 am. *You little shit. Where are you?*
Taylor: 00.34 am. *Eddie called. Are you okay? Text me.*
Taylor: 00.45 am. *Not talking to me? Call, me for God's sake. I'm worried.*
Eddie: 01.00 am. *You are in so much trouble, mister.*
Leslie winced when he read that one.
Taylor: 01.20 am. *Eddie's mad. Me too. Just hope you're okay. Text me ASAP!*

Eddie had called twice; Taylor, too. He didn't listen to the voicemail messages. He knew they'd simply be cursing at him for scaring them.

Leslie sighed and texted back, including them both in his message.

*I'm fine, so sorry, my bad. I'm at Oliver's. Please don't be too mad with me. I forgot 'cos I was BBDIMBF xxoo*

He sniggered as he hit Send. Let them figure that one out. He laid his phone down and pulled the duvet back up. He was only just starting to get comfortable when his phone vibrated crazily. He reached over and picked it up. The Taylor/Eddie conversation was highlighted.

Taylor: *Glad you're okay. You're still in trouble though. All cool with you and Oliver?*

Eddie: *Little bastard. Glad you two made up. About time he got his bloody head on straight.*

Leslie laughed softly. He knew his two friends would still have plenty to say to Oliver when they saw him next about what a prat he'd been for hurting Leslie. He might have to play mediator and make sure his lover wasn't tarred and feathered.

Taylor: *So you were buried balls-deep in the boyfriend, huh? High-five.* There was a picture of a hotdog in a bun attached to the message which Leslie giggled at. He did scowl though. Trust Taylor to have figured that one out.

Eddie: *LOL like that one. I'll have to use it on Gideon*

Taylor: *btw the video you put on YouTube of us singing ABBA songs? You are so dead.*

Leslie laughed loudly then glanced guiltily over at Oliver. He started when he saw that his boyfriend's eyes were open and Oliver was watching him with a lazy smile.

"Sorry I woke you up," Leslie murmured. "It's the guys, they were worried about me. I forgot to text them."

"Do you mind if I see? I'd like to tell them something if I may?" Oliver held out his hand and Leslie passed him the phone. Oliver read through the messages and chuckled when he'd finished.

"They are good guys, aren't they?"

"The best," Leslie agreed.

He watched, a little confused as Oliver texted something, something quite long- winded, then hit Send, gave him back his phone and lay back with a grin.

Leslie read the last outgoing message.

*Thanks for looking out for him, guys. You can beat me up when you see me, I'm ready for you. I'm glad he has friends like you. The Three Houseketeers are now all formally spoken for He's mine now and I promise I'll take care of his heart. I love him. Now if you don't mind, I'm about to be BBDIMBF. Oh and I loved the drunken Dancing Queens. Night chaps*

Leslie's chest beat faster as Oliver reached for him, definite intent on his face and he allowed himself to be drawn down into his boyfriend's loving and passionate embrace. The phone vibrated again but this time, Leslie didn't even bother. He had more important things on his mind.

## ABOUT THE AUTHOR

Susan Mac Nicol is a self-confessed bookaholic, an avid watcher of videos of sexy pole-dancing men, a self-confessed geek and nerd, and in love with her Smartphone. This little treasure is called 'the boyfriend' by her longsuffering husband, who says if it vibrated there'd be no need for him. Susan hasn't had the heart to tell him there's an app for that.

A lover of walks in the forest, theatre productions, dabbling her toes in the cold North Sea and the vibrant city of London where you can experience all four seasons in a day, she is a hater of pantomime (please don't tar and feather her), duplicitous people, bigotry and self-righteous idiots. She likes to think of herself as a 'half full' kind of gal, although sometimes that philosophy is sorely tested.

In an ideal world, Susan Mac Nicol would be Queen of England and banish all the bad people to the Never Never Lands of Wherever-Who Cares. As that's not going to happen, she contents herself with writing her HEA stories and pretending that, just for a little while, good things happen to good people.

**OTHER BOOKS BY SUSAN MAC NICOL**

*Stripped Bare*
*Saving Alexander*
*Worth Keeping*
*Double Alchemy*
*Double Alchemy: Climax*
*Love and Punishment*

THE MEN OF LONDON SERIES

*Love You Senseless*
*Sight & Sinners*

THE STARLIGHT SERIES

*Cassandra by Starlight*
*Together in Starlight*

**Boroughs Publishing Group**

Did you enjoy this book? Drop us a line and say so! We love to hear from readers, and so do our authors. To connect, visit www.boroughspublishinggroup.com online, send comments directly to info@boroughspublishinggroup.com, or friend us on Facebook and Twitter. And be sure to check back regularly for contests and new releases in your favorite subgenres of romance!

Are you an aspiring writer? Check out www.boroughspublishinggroup.com/submit and see if we can help you make your dreams come true.

Made in the USA
Columbia, SC
26 February 2022